*GETTING SENTIMENTAL
OVER YOU*

ACKNOWLEDGEMENTS

Photograph of the *Island Queen* courtesy Cincinnati Historical Library.

"I'll Never Smile Again," Words and Music by Ruth Lowe © Copyright 1939 Universal–MCA Music Publishing, a Division of Universal Studios, Inc. (ASCAP). International Copyright Secured. All Rights Reserved.

"I'm Getting Sentimental over You," by George Bassman and Ned Washington © 1932 (Renewed) EMI Mills Music, Inc. All Rights Reserved. Used by Permission Warner Bros. Publications U. S. Inc., Miami, FL 33014.

"What is This Thing Called Love," by Cole Porter © 1929 (Renewed) Warner Bros. Inc. All Rights Reserved. Used by Permission Warner Bros. Publications U. S. Inc., Miami, FL 33014.

"Violets for Your Furs," by Thomas Adair and Matt Dennis © 1941 (Renewed) by Music Sales Corporation (ASCAP). International Copyright Secured. All Rights Reserved. Reprinted by Permission.

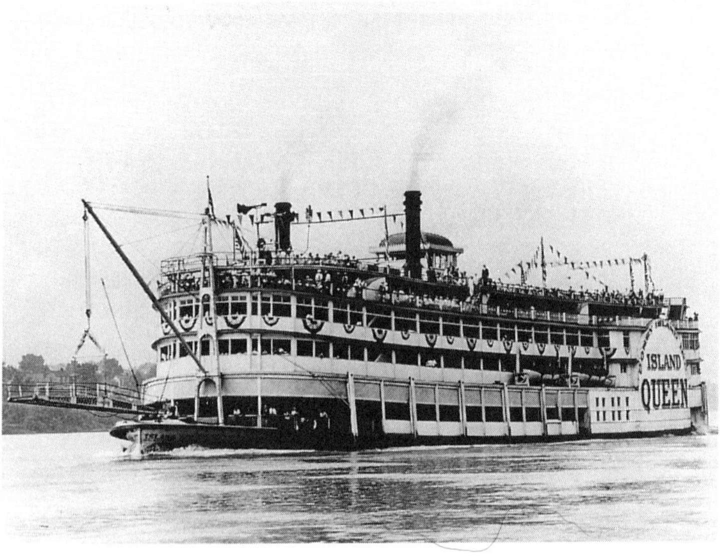
ISLAND
QUEEN

GETTING SENTIMENTAL
OVER YOU

Roger Karshner

NOBLE PORTER PRESS

Copyright © 2002 by Noble Porter Press
All Rights Reserved

Printed in the United States of America

Noble Porter Press, 36-851 Palm View Road
Rancho Mirage, CA 92270

Library of Congress Cataloging-in-publication-Data
Karshner, Roger.
   Getting sentimental over you / Roger Karshner
     p. cm.
   ISBN 0-9634147-4-7 (alk. paper)
    1.   Cincinnati (Ohio)—Fiction.   I. Title
PS3563.A733343 G48 2002
813'054—de21   20022023516

∞This book is printed on paper that meets the requirements of the American Standard of Permanence of paper for printed library material.

PREFACE

During 1988–1990, I desperately searched for a literary vehicle to present as part of my bid for full tenure. I racked my brain. Being a professor of dramatic arts, one would think I would have been capable of writing an original play with facility. Unfortunately, this was not the case. I made several feeble attempts, never getting much farther than Chapter One on the page. I then entertained the notion of writing a scholarly book on Shakespeare's impact upon Freud. This, too, didn't progress much farther than the research stage. I was stymied. Then, as is so often the case, I realized that what I was looking for lay at my doorstep. It was obvious. Why hadn't I thought of it before? And it didn't have a thing to do with theater, Shakespeare, Freud or anything academic at all. It would be a story based upon a long-ago experience in the life of my good neighbor, Noble Johnson.

CHAPTER ONE

DURING *the winter of 1988, I was teaching theater arts at a community college in southern Ohio. The school was located on a beautiful piece of rolling countryside, and—due to its small enrollment and rural location—it had a relaxed, intimate feeling. It wasn't a crowded, impersonal labyrinth like many of the major universities. So I didn't experience the push and shove and pressures that were put upon professors at the bigger institutions. I could teach in an easy way. I could relate to my students on a highly personal basis. It was a good life and my wife, Kristin, a nurse at a clinic in nearby Chillicothe, and I were happy there. Happy, but* financially strapped (professors at small community colleges don't enjoy many gourmet meals). For this reason, I applied for a tenured track position at a large university upstate.

I submitted my résumé and was granted an interview in the spring of that same year. When this went well, I was called back for a meeting with the drama department chair and a subsequent meeting with the search committee, a humorless lot serious about drama. Not that I wasn't. But being overly heavy wasn't my teaching *modus operandi*. I found that this approach had a turn-off effect on my students. Instead, I presented Shakespeare, Molière, Ibsen, and the big boys in a more casual fashion, assigning them importance without becoming intellectually abstruse. I presented them as playwrights, not gods. And I refuted the notion that great plays were deep mysteries couched in enigmas. It was a matter of finding the truth in the play scripts. It was all in the script. When I explained this and my methods to the committee, they listened intently, respectfully. Then, Professor Hayes, a buttoned-up type, asked, "What's your understanding of Brecht?" (Academics are irrevocably hung up on Brecht

3
Getting Sentimental over You

and Ionesco, and every major theater arts department in the country has done *Rhinoceros* to death.) I was inclined to give a political answer, but I opted for the truth (anything less meant I'd be placing myself in a position of having to do *Mother Courage*, *Baal*, and *The Caucasian Chalk Circle* every year for the rest of my life).

"Well . . . to be perfectly honest, I don't think Brecht understood Brecht."

There was a vast silence. Then Hayes smiled, coming unbuttoned a bit. He looked at the others and said, "I think he'll do just fine." I was to start in the fall.

With the new position came a considerable increase in salary and, of course, the possibility of full tenure. This, and the fact that Kris had found a good job with the local hospital, meant we could finally afford our own home. So that summer we shopped around our future city, looking for something we could afford. As is usually the case, we fell in love with a place that was over our budget. But it felt warm. Friendly. It was us. So, budget aside, we bought it. It was an older, two-story frame house in an established residential section near the campus; an area once considered the *crème de la crème* of the city. Although now considered second banana to the newer sections of the north side, it was still a respectable neighborhood.

The summer of '88 was unusually hot and humid, the kind of humidity that "could really sweat a man," as my father used to say. And on our moving day it seemed as though the Good Lord had ordered up an extra helping of perspiration. We couldn't afford a moving company, so we moved ourselves in a large van I'd rented from U-Haul. It was amazing what the two of us had accumulated since our wedding. Little things, odds and ends, had multiplied and found their way into our lives, attaching themselves like barnacles to the hull of our existence. So finding room for everything was no mean task. But with the help of friends, we squeezed it all in, cramming the van to the roof and filling our Honda Civic. Early the following morning we said our good-byes and headed out on Route 35 like motorized pioneers; me in the van, Kris in the Civic behind.

It was on this day we met Noble Johnson.

CHAPTER TWO

AUGUST 2, 1988

THERE *was no fanfare, handshake, or prefatory conversation. Suddenly there was just his presence lightening the end of a mattress I was struggling to remove from the back of the van; a strong, lanky presence insinuating itself into the moment with a smile and a nod.*

"Thanks a lot."

"These mattresses can be pretty tricky."

That was it. Beyond this, except for a brief swap of identities and an occasional monosyllabic exchange, there was no conversation. The man was just there, helping out, being the quintessential good neighbor. And thank heaven for his help. Without it, moving the heavier pieces—the couch, mattresses, appliances—would have been a monumental task.

While moving the heavy pieces was the more taxing job, it was handling the smaller items that consumed the most time. While bringing in an armload of these, Mr. Johnson dropped a small wooden box containing love letters written by Kris and me. It was a small replica of a cedar chest that Kris had had for years. One hinge was broken, as was the tiny hasp that had at one time secured its top. When the packets of ribbon-wrapped letters tumbled from the box, Mr. Johnson was embarrassed and contrite.

Kris reassured him as she gathered the letters and returned them to the chest. "Please. No problem. They're love letters Rog and I exchanged during college. That's one of the other nice things about them—they're not breakable."

Noble Johnson was our salvation that day, staying until each piece of furniture had been strategically arranged to Kristin's satisfaction. So by dusk the job was completed. We were settled. We were in. Everything was in place,

7
Getting Sentimental over You

nothing was missing. Nothing, we realized, except Noble Johnson, who had disappeared as unceremoniously as he had arrived.

"When did he leave, Kris?"

"I don't know. Some time ago, I guess."

"He didn't even give us time to thank him."

"That's terrible."

"We'll have to go over."

"Oh, yeah. Right away."

"I don't know what we'd have done without him. A nice man."

"Yes. Very. Strange, though . . . "

"Strange?"

"Yes."

"How do you mean?"

"I don't know. It's hard to explain."

"He didn't seem strange to me."

"Then . . . you didn't notice?"

I didn't have the slightest idea what she was getting at.

"Notice what?"

"The way he kept staring at me."

"Oh, come on now. You don't mean that—"

"No, no . . . Nothing like that. Nothing lecherous, or anything. It was like . . ."

"Yeah?"

"I don't know. It's just that it gave me a strange feeling. It was like he was photographing me, or something. Weird." She shivered slightly.

"I think you've inhaled too much seltzer."

"Maybe. But I didn't imagine it."

Just then there was a gentle rap on the screen door.

"Who could that be?"

"Beats me. Our creditors couldn't have found us this fast."

It was Noble Johnson. Through the screen he presented a matted portrait. He was smiling. His mouth was expressive and wide. His eyes were warm and brown and spoke to you softly, inviting you inside. Although he wasn't young, there was a youthfulness about him that belied his years. He was lean and trim and his forearms were muscular and rippled sinuously when he moved his fingers. But the most distinguishing thing about him was a projection of gentleness, an aura of kindness that put you at ease in his presence.

"I figured maybe you and the wife would like to come on over for some lemonade."

The man was too good to be true. He'd just

Getting Sentimental over You

spent the good part of the day helping us move and now here he was offering refreshments.

"Who is it, dear?"

"Our savior—Mr. Johnson."

"Come on over, you two. It's a nice evening. We'll sit out under the magnolia tree. See you in a few minutes."

He turned and left the porch, disappearing lithely beyond the outlines of a sagging wisteria. I returned to the living room. "Can you believe this guy? I don't know who lives on the other side of us, but if they're half as neat as this man, we've gone to heaven without dying. He wants us to come over for lemonade. Can you believe it?"

Kris pushed herself from a properly angled chair.

"Give me a minute to slap on some makeup."

"Who's going to see you? Anyway, you're almost pretty the way you are."

"Get lost, professor."

After I'd slipped into a fresh shirt and Kris had reworked her makeup, we walked over to Noble Johnson's place. His house was next door and connected to ours by a wide lawn. A slight breeze was blowing and thin, dark clouds were edging their way across the sky. Noble was sitting in one of four metal lawn chairs, the kind you would see fronting tourist cabins and service stations back in the forties and fifties. He was rocking gently under the low branches of a sprawling magnolia tree whose white, translucent flowers were giving off the best of nature's perfume. Near him, on a small, metal stand, was a pitcher of lemonade and three plastic glasses. He appeared relaxed and perfectly suited to the moment as though he'd been painted in.

"Si' down." He motioned to the chairs and we sat. "There's nothing quite like lemonade on a warm evening."

"I couldn't agree more," Kris said.

"And sitting out under a nice tree. Learned that from my father. He always said, 'On a hot day, find yourself a nice shade tree and sit.'"

"Your father was a smart man," Kris said.

"And gets smarter every day."

Kris looked about, admiring the setting. "My, what a lovely spot."

"It's my little bit of heaven."

We seated ourselves.

11
Getting Sentimental over You

"Mr. Johnson—"

"Noble."

"Noble, Roger and I can't thank you enough for your help today. We don't know what we would have done without you."

"She's right."

"The woman's always right. Remember that, Rog."

"Now this is my kind of man," Kris said.

Our laughter was underscored by the low rumble of distant thunder. Mr. Johnson poured lemonade into the tall, plastic glasses. His movements were precise and graceful.

"Helping out gave me something to do today. Anyway, I like to keep busy."

I couldn't help but ask. "You're still working?"

"Oh, no. But I keep my hand in. I was a shop teacher at one of our junior highs till I retired a few years back. Now I do volunteer work. With kids. They like to work with their hands. And it keeps me involved. Too many people my age vegetate when they stop working. They retire to dying." He handed us each a glass.

"Is Mrs. Johnson joining us?" It was a natural thing for me to assume.

He hesitated, glass in hand. "There isn't a Mrs. Johnson. Never married." Then, dismissing the subject casually, he raised his glass. "Well . . . here's to good neighbors."

"The best," I said.

We drank long. The cooling citrus was refreshing and brought back childhood memories of wide verandas and endless lawns and recalled to me how my mother used to make lemonade on hot days. She'd cut the lemons into slices and place them in the bottom of an old, metal pitcher. Then she'd pour in scoopfuls of sugar and grind it into the lemons before filling the pitcher with water. I hadn't had fresh lemonade in years. It wasn't the kind of thing people took time with in these days of quick-dispenser fixes of Pepsi and Coke. I'd forgotten about lemonade's cooling effect, its ability to soothe in an almost tranquilizing way.

"I like to sit out here in the evening. I like to watch the cars go by." His place, like ours and the others on the block, was a two-story frame house that had been built in the late 30s. The homes were situated far back from the street and fronted by gentle sloping terraces. "This old magnolia's been here as long as I have."

13
Getting Sentimental over You

"It's beautiful," Kris said. She looked up under the network of flowered limbs. It was a lovely, comforting thing—a glowing halo over our heads.

"Started it from a slip back in 1950. Look at it now." He looked up at it admiringly. It was an old friend. "I've been all around the country and this is the best place I know for a person to unwind. You sit out here, there's no time. There's a kind of eternity under these branches." He spoke between sips in a slow, measured baritone. "It's the simple things, you know. The little, everyday pleasures. The give and take between old friends. Special memories." He hesitated. "Like those love letters of yours."

We exchanged glances at this. It seemed odd he would bring up the letters. Odd and provocative. But we said nothing. Nothing is the best thing to say during moments of awkwardness.

"I owe you an apology, Mrs. Warner."

"Kris, please. An apology?"

"Yes."

"I don't know what for. For dropping the letters? Like I said, they're not breakable."

"No. For the way I was staring at you today."

She did her best to avoid the issue. "Staring?"

"Yes."

"Why, I didn't notice . . . I mean there certainly wasn't any— "

He didn't allow for embarrassed fumbling. "Please. Don't pretend you didn't notice. I saw the look on your face. And I don't blame you. It was rude of me. But it's just that . . . that you remind me so much of someone else. The resemblance is uncanny. So please don't take offense. Besides, she was beautiful."

"Well . . . I can hardly take offense then, can I?"

"I just wanted you to know, that's all. I didn't want you to get the wrong idea. But seeing you today . . . it brought back a lotta memories."

"Good, I hope."

"Oh, yes."

"Well, then . . ."

"Just seeing you, the way you moved, well . . . Let me ask you, are you a good dancer?"

"Not when I'm her partner," I said.

15
Getting Sentimental over You

"Not really. Pretty clumsy, actually."

"Dancing's a great thing."

Kris leaned forward, eyeing him in a penetrating way. "I'm not, but I've got a feeling you are."

"Make that *was*. But I haven't danced in years. But, at one time, if I must say so, I was pretty darned good." He rocked, causing the metal chair to bob slightly. "Of course we had ballrooms back then. All over the place. And your big bands."

"Oh, I love that music. What a relief from what we have now. Like Roger says, today it all sounds like sheetmetal work."

"So, you like the sounds of the big bands, huh? Well, now . . . we'll have to do something about that."

He excused himself and moved off into his house. A few moments later, music of the 40s drifted into the dusk. Filtered through the screens of the Johnson property, it lent a romantic mood to our little scene of magnolia and lemonade. I wasn't a student of the music of that era, but I could appreciate it in contrast to what they were playing now. It wasn't raucous. It wasn't profane. It didn't contain a strained sense of urgency. And there was melody.

When Noble returned from his house, he was accompanied by the trombone strains of "I'm Getting Sentimental over You," its melody delivered silkily, soaring on shimmering wings. The music drifted out over the evening, softening the borders of the encroaching night. It brought with it a sense of weightlessness, suspending the moment in time. It seemed as though everything had stopped to listen, to appreciate the seamless beauty of the sound. And in the distance, soft thunder gave the impression of applause, as if the gods were giving an ovation to the man with the golden horn.

With him Noble had brought a well-worn cigar box, its label indistinguishable due to handling over time. Its lid was secured by a wide rubber band. He held the box lovingly, gently, as if it were a fragile, living thing. One could sense that this old box held treasures. Kris and I watched our neighbor as he absorbed the music and whatever thoughts it evoked. We were silent. Conversation, any disruption, would have been impertinent at a moment so pure, would have been an obscene intrusion into feelings so obviously in the air. Even the

Getting Sentimental over You

light tinkling of the ice in our drinks seemed to insinuate itself harshly.

I set my glass aside.

CHAPTER THREE

WE *continued to sit in silence as the music spun out into the night, until the record had concluded.*

"That was Tommy Dorsey. One of the greats. Nobody had a sound like Dorsey. You never heard 'im take a breath. Had some great bands. Especially this one. Had great sidemen: Ziggy Elman, Joe Bushkin, Hymie Shertzer, Don Lodice, Buddy Rich—great players. He used to play all of the major ballrooms. This was back in the late 30s and early 40s, back before TV killed the country. We had some nice ballrooms: Lakeside Park in Dayton, Moonlight

19
Getting Sentimental over You

Terrace at Indian Lake, and Moonlite Gardens at Coney Island—a big amusement park that was up the river about ten miles outta Cincinnati. You could ride a boat all the way from Cincy to Coney—the *Island Queen*. She was a steel-constructed, side-paddle-wheeler. Very elegant. They always had a good local band on board: Barney Rapp or Clyde Trask—house bands. Barney Rapp kind of discovered Doris Kappelhoff and got her to change her name to Day.

"Cincy was great for music. The Clooney sisters—Betty and Rosie—who were from Maysville, Kentucky, worked at WLW. Great singers who later went with the Tony Pastor Band. You'd leave Cincy from the public landing and drink and dance your way all the way up to Coney. I got to know one of the trumpet players with the Rapp outfit—Norm Hathaway. He worked at 'LW, too. Nice guy. Once in a while he'd sneak me onto the *Queen* as a band member. I really appreciated it. I was just a young fella with snappy clothes, romance on my mind and not a heck of a lot in my pocket.

"You'd leave Cincy in the afternoon—the boat would be packed; it held up to 4,000 people—and by the time you got to Coney Island you'd danced so much your feet would be too hot for your shoes. Then, at Coney, you'd picnic and ride the rides and drink beer till you became German. But the big time was at night, when you'd dance under the stars at Moonlite. To a big band. Especially the name bands. And they all came to Coney, one time or other, all of 'em: Dorsey, Miller, Shaw, Sammy Kaye, Benny Goodman, Les Brown—you name 'em. The dance floor would be packed. It was great. Let me tell you, you've never really heard this music till you've heard it played live. Then, after dancing all night, you'd ride the boat back to Cincinnati."

"It must have been something," Kris said.

"Even when it was hot, it was always cool on the river. And coming into Cincy at night was a real sight. The town would be all lit up like a Christmas tree with its reflection shimmering in the water." He halted briefly. "*The Island Queen* burned up back in late '42. Oil tanks exploded."

"That's a shame," Kris said.

"I guess. I don't know. Maybe kinda fitting, in a way."

21
Getting Sentimental over You

"How's that?" I asked.

"The era—the dancing, the big bands—was going to come to an end anyhow. Maybe the boat knew what was coming, was way ahead of the curve. If it hadn't burned, it would have wound up being a sad, floating reminder of another time, an old wreck rusting in the Ohio River."

Kris looked at him wistfully. "Sad."

"I guess. But things move on. Except me, maybe. I still miss the era. The good times. People. Friends. Guess I'm just an old dinosaur."

He was old, certainly, but there was nothing old about him. He still possessed the same remarkable, youthful quality I had noticed that afternoon. He sat erect, head back. His hair, while streaked with gray, was full and lustrous. He was exceedingly neat. His freshly laundered denim shirt was tucked carefully into a trim, chino waistline.

"You'll never be old. You look great."

"Well . . . I suddenly felt old today when I saw your wife. Seeing her opened up a lotta things reminding me of the past."

"God, don't tell me I look like the 40s."

He reassured her that she didn't. "No no, nothing like that. You just took me back, that's all. Your resemblance to someone. Then . . . when the love letters fell out. . . ."

There was what seemed an interminable interlude. We sat silently. What do you say at a moment like this? Nothing. You just wait. So, we waited.

He finally said, "Then, when you said you loved the music. . . Know what? I haven't played that album in I don't know how long."

"But you love it," Kris said.

"Yes. But some memories are just too hard to deal with. So you push 'em back, keep 'em below the surface. I not only don't play the record, I never talk like this to anyone. Anyone. That's what's so amazing about this evening. Something's in the air. You know, I've lived next to Mrs. Granger on the other side for forty years, and all she knows about me is that I'm a retired shop teacher with a nice magnolia tree. But today, seeing you . . . the letters . . . the feelings here tonight . . . it's crazy. All of a sudden, I just had to open up. I knew this afternoon this was going to be a very unusual day."

Getting Sentimental over You

"For us, too," I said.

"Kris, seeing you has taken me back forty-six years. Here, let me show you something."

He placed his glass carefully on the table and placed the cigar box on his knees. He removed the wide rubber band. There was a period of hesitation as he gazed at the box with an expression of trepidation, as though folding back its lid could result in some calamity of major consequence. His fingers hovered over the box, quivering slightly. Finally he turned back the lid slowly, as if not wishing to disturb something sleeping within. Inside was what appeared to be letters and scraps of memorabilia. He fingered the contents gingerly, routing carefully through it. He removed two small items and handed them to Kris, who passed them to me: two ticket stubs, worn, their once-gaudy colors faded, torn by an unknown hand. I slid the stubs between my fingers, noting the faded print:

ADMIT ONE
MOONLITE GARDENS
SUNDAY, AUGUST 2, 1942
THE TOMMY DORSEY BAND

I handed the stubs back to him. He returned them to the box, closed its lid, and placed it carefully on the metal stand.

"That's a long time ago," I said.

"Yes. Did you notice the date?"

"August 2, 1942."

"That's today's date," Kris said.

"Like I said. I knew this was going to be a very unusual day."

I looked over at Kris, who was as much in the dark as I was. "Well, Kris, it looks like we're in the middle of something here."

"I'm sorry, I didn't mean to make it sound so mysterious. But all of the elements—the letters, your wife, the date—it's just all so coincidental. Or maybe not. Maybe there's something behind it."

"You mean, supernatural?"

"No, no. Nothing like that. But sometimes things happen, you know. Things you just can't explain. The planets are aligned just right, something in the wind, the moment—who knows? And today, after all these years . . . well, today something happened."

You couldn't blame Kris for asking. "Would

25
Getting Sentimental over You

it be asking too much of you to tell us what?"

He looked at her for a moment. Or through her, because at that moment she didn't exist. I didn't exist. He appeared to be fixed upon something distant, something outside the moment, something elusive and deep and impenetrable. The silence was long and uncomfortable. Maybe we'd gone too far. Perhaps Kris had stepped over the line with her question.

Then, after what seemed an interminable period, he came back into focus and began to speak. His story was captivating.

CHAPTER FOUR

AUGUST 2, 1942

*I*N *his one-bedroom apartment on Cincinnati's north side, Noble Johnson stood and cleared away his breakfast dishes. On a nearby stand, an old Majestic radio was crackling "Violets for Your Furs." "And it was spring for a while, remember . . ." Noble hummed along as he casually scraped food into a colander, looking out his kitchen window at Sunday as it gained momentum in pursuit of noon. He then washed the dishes, dried them, and placed them precisely in a cupboard above the sink. The apartment, while humble, was*

Getting Sentimental over You

spotless, everything in its place. Though Spartan and certainly not lavishly appointed, the place still had a bit of style, its inexpensive furniture reflecting masculine good taste. If it were possible to read a person by the appearance of his surroundings, one would conclude (correctly) that Noble Johnson was a discerning person of considerable neatness.

After finishing up in the kitchen, he bathed. Then shaved. He painted on a heavy layer of Colgate lather with his shaving brush, then removed it precisely, rolling it back in narrow rows with his Gillette single-edged razor. Easy at the sideburns. They must be sharp and even. Careful under the nose and up the neck. There was no tolerance for a nick on this special day. The blade was pulled with careful ease through the creamy curtain, pulling it aside, exposing the man beneath. His eyes were brown and wide-set, and they shone with a soft intelligence over high cheekbones. His hair, naturally chestnut, was sunburned to the color of caramel. While handsome, he wasn't handsome in an 8 x 10 glossy way. His handsomeness was a reflection of character and quality and resolve. What he was—decisive, strong, at ease in his skin—stood out all over him like an advertisement. After shaving, he rinsed and patted Bay Rum on his cheeks, shuddering slightly as the alcohol burned his blade-agitated skin. He then applied a spot of Brilliantine to the palm of his hand, transferred it to his hair, and rubbed it in briskly with his fingertips, bringing a high shine to the taffy-brown strands. A precise parting and combing completed the job. He turned from side to side, critically eyeing the final product in his bathroom mirror. The mirror liked what it saw. He passed inspection.

His small bedroom contained the possessions of which he was most proud, aside from his precious Ford roadster: his clothing. Many pairs of pants were hung neatly on a long dowel running across the bottom of the closet. Above, jackets and shirts were arrayed regimentally. On the top shelf, neatly arranged boxes held his shoe collection. The boxes had been boldly labeled according to style: white bucks, brown loafers, black loafers, wing tips, suedes, brown and white two-tones, black and white two-tones, black oxfords, tan cap-toes, saddles. He studied the closet, pulling at his Bay Rumed face gently with his long fingers.

29
Getting Sentimental over You

His undershirt accentuated his broad shoulders and the muscular taper of his back. After a few seconds of serious consideration, he removed his wardrobe *du jour*. He dressed quickly, moving easily to the Latin beat of "Amour," which was being air-mailed from the old Majestic. As he threaded an alligator belt through the loops of his trousers, he studied a photograph of his parents on his dresser.

Taken on their wedding day at his grandparents' home in Springdale, Ohio, it was a picture of a happy, smiling couple, arm in arm under an arbor of spring-blooming honeysuckle. He reflected upon their moment, attempting to place himself in the scene as a member of the wedding party, become an observer at this long-ago event now living only in an ornate pewter frame. How had it been between them on that day? What were their dreams and aspirations? He lifted the photo from the dresser and studied closely his mother's upturned face with its look of loving adulation, and his father's stance of relaxed rectitude that would one day be genetically imprinted on him. He thought of their married lifetime (one that had produced him, his brother, and sister) and tried to imagine the hardships, trials and triumphs, the vicissitudes and victories that had taken place over their long, enduring union. How'd they done it? What was their secret? It was an elusive thing to contemplate. He couldn't imagine himself committed to a lifetime with any woman. It was a far-distant consideration for a guy of twenty-one with a choice of girls, a sharp Ford roadster, and a shoe collection rivaling any in Cincinnati. He replaced the photo with care, returning the mystery to his dresser, where it would remain unsolved, its answer buried within the fading black-and-white wedding picture snapped a lifetime of events ago.

From the top drawer of the dresser he removed money-clipped cash and two garishly colorful tickets:

ADMIT ONE
MOONLITE GARDENS
SUNDAY, AUGUST 2, 1942
THE TOMMY DORSEY BAND

The carefully accoutered Noble Johnson stepped from his apartment into a neighbor-

Getting Sentimental over You

hood that was predominately German. Much of Cincinnati was German. Because of this, the city had excellent German restaurants and good local breweries: Burger, Huedepohl, Schoenling, and Weideman, Burger being the largest with a big, sprawling plant just off Paddock Road.

Noble always knew when the Burger plant was operating because, from his apartment, he could smell the sweet-sour fumes generated by smoldering barley and hops. But there were no fumes on this day because it was Sunday, and Sunday was a day of rest. People respected the Sabbath back in 1942. Sunday meant relaxing with family and leisurely drives in the country or down along the Ohio River, which rolled along sluggishly as if it were reluctant to mix blood with the Mississippi. Sunday was always a quiet day and it was difficult to find anything open around town, save an occasional gas station or neighborhood grocery store.

This suited Noble Johnson just fine. Six days working at the Chevy plant in Norwood were plenty. (The plant had been hastily converted to the war effort and was running three shifts around the clock, grinding out munitions to support the armed forces.) It was often necessary for Noble to work double shifts or take up the slack when a co-worker was ill or otherwise unable to be on the line. But he didn't mind. America was at war. It was a privilege, a patriotic duty to sacrifice for the greater good. For this was a righteous cause. There was clarity. Forces of evil were at work. The purpose was clear. A sense of patriotism gripped the country and bled over the states into the life of every citizen.

On a front porch across the street, a neighbor—wearing the front-porch Sunday attire of a five o'clock shadow and undershirt—was reading the *Enquirer.* He waved.

"You're up bright and early."

"Yep."

"Can't wait to get to church, huh, Noble?"

"What about you? What's your excuse?"

"I have to stay home and catch up on current events." He rattled the *Enquirer* in the air. "Besides, my wife has enough religion for the both of us. Where you off to?"

"Coney."

"Again?"

"Every chance I get."

"Well . . . you're sure dressed for it."

33
Getting Sentimental over You

Indeed he was. A brown and gray loafer jacket over a tan sport shirt buttoned at the neck. Brown and white two-tone shoes. Argyle socks. Powder-blue, tropical-worsted gabardine trousers. In the light of day his Brilliantined hair took on a shiny radiance. Every element of appearance had been ritualistically attended to in order to present young Noble Johnson in the most attractive way. And an attractive package it was. Suitable for framing. Being over six feet and athletically built, he wore his clothes well. The loafer jacket hung at ease over his big shoulders and draped loosely, swinging casually as he bounced down the steps from his apartment.

"Tommy Dorsey's playing tonight."

"T.D., huh? Wow! If it wasn't for the old lady, I'd go along with ya. But she'd never let me loose up there with all them bobby-soxers."

As if you'd have a chance, Noble thought. "Yeah. Sure."

The day was bright and the roofs of the row houses stood out regimentally against a clear Cincinnati sky. Along the block there was little coming and going. Small children, looking too clean for children, walked past on their way to mass (the area was heavily Catholic). Noble smiled at them, and they returned his greeting with faces scrubbed to a shine, their youthful laughter diminishing to a distant wind-chime as they moved down the street. They were happy, carefree, and oblivious to the fact that the German blitzkrieg was rolling into the Kuban and overrunning Voroshilovsk, that the P-47 Thunderbolt was now in production, that General Andrei Yeremenko had been sent to defend Stalingrad, that Dr. Irmfried Eberl was overseeing the "final solution" at Treblinka Concentration Camp, that Australian troops were losing the battle in the jungles of New Guinea. In their mood of Sunday celebration, there was no room for war.

The 1936 Ford roadster was navy blue with red-rimmed wheels. It was Noble's proudest possession. It was small and sleek and sporty and, without fail, prompted the question, "How fast will she go?" Although second-hand, the car was in excellent condition due to the mother-like coddling it received at the loving hands of Mr. Noble Johnson, Esquire. "Motorists Wise Simonize."

He unsnapped the hasps securing the top

Getting Sentimental over You

and folded it back into the space provided behind the seat, pushing it down snugly into the opening. The car was now racy and the perfect complement to a good-looking fellow in a new loafer jacket and two-tone shoes.

Noble started the car and it rumbled to life, settling into a smooth V-8 purr. As he pulled from the curb, he snapped on its Crosley radio to WLW ("The Nation's Station"), a megakillowatt operation that threw its signal into every corner of America.

Peter Grant was broadcasting war and local news in a voice as resonant as thunder, his sonorous tones rattling the radio's cheap speaker: in the Pacific, U.S. Marines were grouping for the invasion of Guadalcanal. The German war machine was still in high gear in Europe. In Townsville, Australia, they were bracing for what was expected to be a last stand. Three men were arrested in Newport, Kentucky, for the murder of a Monmouth Street merchant. Last night, Frank McCormick had blasted one over the 387 foot, center field wall at Crosley Field.

The war news was pertinent to Noble due to his age and eligibility. The only thing keeping him from foreign shores was his defense job. And even this was fragile shelter. As the conflict wore on, Uncle Sam would be calling up more able-bodied men. Many of Noble's friends had already enlisted or been drafted. The war was a prevalent, insinuating thing. And Noble was torn. Even though he was doing work critical to the war effort, he often felt, in view of the sacrifices many of his buddies were making on foreign shores, that this wasn't enough.

Peter Grant's rounded vowels gave way to Glenn Miller's "A String of Pearls." The arrangement—incorporating the trademark clarinet lead—filled the roadster and put Noble in that "Miller Mood." He tapped his fingers rhythmically to the tune. The music was not only perfect for the moment, it was also a sedative for anxieties generated by the daily news. Then came "Opus One," "Begin the Beguine," "Woodchopper's Ball," "Tuxedo Junction." Happy music all in a row. It swung. Then came "Stardust," "At Last," "These Foolish Things." Romantic music all in a row. It soothed. The sounds of the big bands and balladeers were perfect accompaniment to the V-8 as it throbbed along in tempo up Spring Grove Avenue.

CHAPTER FIVE

AUDRY McClure was angora sweaters and the fresh scent of Camay. She was vibrant and beautiful and was expert in the personal application of the cosmetics she sold at her job at McAlpin's Department Store. Her skin was the texture of cashmere—soft, as if it had been kept under wraps since birth. Her long, chestnut-brown hair melted over her shoulders in thick, silken layers. When she walked, she swayed to a personal cadence that set her skirts swinging recklessly about her attractive legs. Her grayish-green eyes were alert, her pouty lips glistened sensuously under a bright Cody glaze. Her features were softly rounded as if they'd been sculpted, rethought, and sculpted some more. Nature had taken great care in her creation.

She lived in the Clifton area in a middle-class home with a nice side yard. There were shade trees and fruit trees and an arbor with grape vines growing over it. In summer, the grapes would ripen and hang heavily from the vines like large bundles of purple marbles. Under the arbor was a wooden bench where one could sit, think, talk, make love, or do absolutely nothing at all.

Audry and Noble had met at Hughes High School and had gone steady during their senior year. After graduating, their romance cooled and they chose independence. But they remained close and dated often.

Audry wasn't the only girl in Noble's life, but she was special. Not simply because she was spectacular (which she undoubtedly was). Not because of her skirts that swung about her Hollywood legs. Not because of her pastel-rainbow collection of angora sweaters that softly complemented the rolling firmness of her sky-pointing breasts. No. Even though these alluring facets could not to be overlooked, they were not central to the cut of this precious

Getting Sentimental over You

stone, the thing that gave it its luster and desirability. It was the fact that she was the best dancer in all of Cincinnati.

On the dance floor she was the best. A natural. She knew all of the latest dances, to which she applied her magic, making the jitterbug, fox trot, tango, and waltz her original works of art. She was, undeniably, unquestionably, Cincinnati's Swing Era Terpsichore. And this, coupled with her radiant sexuality and her youthful vitality, accounted for her great popularity. To be seen on the dance floor with Audry McClure was validation of one's dancing abilities because Audry would never take the floor with less than a competent partner, one who could match her sense of rhythm and creativity. This was the reason she was frequently seen dancing with Noble Johnson at Moonlite Gardens, Castle Farm, and the chic Terrace Café, with its tuxedoed waiters and impressive ice sculpture at the Netherland Plaza downtown. The '36 roadster and the fact that he was handsome were certainly factors, but had he not been an able dance partner, he would have never enjoyed the pleasure of her company for anything more than an occasional movie followed by an obligatory hot fudge sundae at Graeter's Ice Cream Parlor. Dancing came first and foremost for Audry McClure. Dancing ruled.

When Noble pulled into her driveway, she was waiting for him at her door. He killed the engine, cut short Artie Shaw's "Frenesi," and made his way to the house. Audry joined him on the porch.

"I tried to catch you before you left."

"Oh, yeah? How come?"

"I can't go."

"Can't go? Whadaya mean, you can't go?"

"I can't go."

"C'mon. You gotta be kidding?"

Her expression said otherwise. She took his hands, pulling him close. "It's my aunt. Up in Oxford. She's had a stroke, or something."

"Oh, man!"

"It was unexpected. Mom and Dad had to go up. So, I have to stay here and watch Harold." The name Harold left her lips as though it were bad medicine.

"But this is Tommy Dorsey, Aud, you can't miss this. I mean—"

"I know. I know. Please. Don't remind me."

"Can't you get someone else?"

Getting Sentimental over You

"I've tried. I've called everybody. No good. I'm sorry."

"I can't believe this." His disappointment was obvious.

"Hey! You think you're the only one disappointed here? I'd die to dance to that band. I've been looking forward to it for weeks. And now I've got to stay home and take care of my brat brother. I hate him!" She slammed a loafer to the porch floor, accenting her remark.

"Not half as much as I do." He pulled the tickets from his jacket pocket. "Well . . . may as well deep-six these." He made a motion as if to tear them in two.

She seized his arm. "No, no! Don't do that! That's nuts! Don't be crazy. You go on by yourself."

"I can't do that."

"Sure you can."

"What's the point?"

"The point is, you get to hear T.D. That's the point."

"Naw. It wouldn't be right."

"Look. There's no sense in both of us being miserable. And you sure don't wanna hang around here all day."

"It wouldn't be that bad."

"With my brat brother? You kidding? You'd wanna choke him after two hours."

He hadn't given great thought to the demon lurking within. "Well . . . "

"He'd drive you crazy."

"You sure you don't mind?"

"Of course I'll mind. You kidding? But it'd be silly to waste those tickets."

"But it won't be the same. I mean, hanging around Moonlite all alone. I'll feel like a dope."

Harold's voice came from within, an annoying, high-pitched demand. "Aud-ree!"

"Shut up! See what I mean? You'd be outta your mind by noon."

"I sure don't envy you. Spending all day around here with that guy."

"I'd like to break his neck."

"You sure you don't mind if I go up alone?"

"It'd be crazy if you didn't."

"Well . . . okay."

"Gimme a call later tonight. Fill me in. Okay?"

"Okay . . . but I'm sure gonna miss the dancing."

"Hey! What about me?"

Getting Sentimental over You

"C'mon. I'll miss you a whole lot more than the dancing. You know that, Aud." But he really wouldn't. He would miss her because, when they danced, he was swept into another rapturous dimension. With her in his arms, he was transported to a place outside time and space where reality and fantasy became one. When Noble Johnson danced with Audry McClure, he was Fred Astaire.

CHAPTER SIX

As he backed from her driveway, she was waving weakly, a picture of abandonment, obviously heavy with thoughts of boredom and responsibility for an obnoxious nine-year-old. While he would be at Coney Island enjoying the music and fun, she would be languishing in the chintzy confines of her Clifton prison with a fractious jailer named Harold. And Noble would be languishing, too. When the music began, he would be without a partner, on the sidelines, nothing more than a fashionable statue. While the band played and dancers swayed to "The Sentimental Gentleman of Swing," he would be merely a well-groomed spectator. But at least he'd be there, on the scene, in the presence of great music. Which was much better than a night in front of his radio listening to Waite Hoyt broadcast the Cincinnati Reds. So all wasn't lost. Even though he and Audry wouldn't be dazzling the wallflowers, he would be spending an evening under the stars at Moonlite with the Tommy Dorsey Band.

As the convertible spun down Vine Street, its radio spilled "Opus One," "Skylark," and Bob Eberle intoned "At Last." A persistent breeze caressed Noble's hair, tempting it, tugging, coaxing, but not convincing enough in its argument (it would have taken a major debate) to overcome the resistance of the well-oiled strands. His fastidiousness was impenetrable, a fortress against any invader. It defied all comers.

Vine Street descended sharply into the city, requiring Noble to brake the Ford frequently. At Third Street, he turned east to Broadway, then turned south on Broadway in the direction of the river. The drive made him feel important, cosmopolitan. He always felt this way when he drove through the downtown area—elevated and special. After all, he was just a blue-collar guy from the north side, he wasn't one of the people who worked downtown: bankers, brokers, lawyers, merchants, professional men, local movers and shakers who talked business over martinis at La Normandie while he was sitting over his lunch pail at Chevy. Being downtown for them was nothing; for Noble it was always an event.

On summer Sundays people came from all over to be on and near the Ohio. It was a great river, and its eternal movement, its timeless lapping against the shore, its slow eddies and gentle tides, its romantic connection to the great riverboats that hauled goods and people as America moved ever outward, conjured the past and sparked the imagination. And it always seemed cooler at the river, even during the long, hot, humid days. Cooler and more restful.

Noble parked near the Broadway landing and made his way among the crowd to the *Island Queen*. The steamer, a side-wheeler, was an inviting thing. Long and graceful with five brightly painted decks, she rested regally at the dock, preening, as if showing herself off to the

Getting Sentimental over You

city. Her tall, twin stacks emitted tendrils of thin, black smoke. There was a steady hiss of steam and an occasional, muted rumble from the oil-fired boilers located near her paddle wheels aft. She presented a nostalgic picture of riverboat finery, evoking romantic notions of southern belles, sly-eyed gamblers, and antebellum days.

Noble purchased a ticket and boarded the *Queen* along with picnickers with pregnant baskets, and children excited as only children can be. The boat was quickly filling. On the ballroom deck the band could be heard playing "Muskrat Ramble."

Noble purchased a draft beer (served in a large, waxen, paper cup) and a soft pretzel. He slathered a thick coating of yellow mustard on the pretzel. The pretzel was warm and salty and was made deliciously tart by the mustard. He washed down his first bite with a long drink of beer that left a small, white crescent on his upper lip and a cooling, satisfying, burnt-sour aftertaste on his tongue.

By the time he reached the ballroom deck, people were already dancing. He took a place near the bandstand and waved his pretzel at trumpeter Norm Hathaway, who returned his greeting as the band was making a flawless segue into "Beale Street Blues." Across the river, on the Kentucky side, the cities of Newport and Covington appeared to be moving as the Queen rolled on waves created by passing speedboats.

Both Newport and Covington were visited frequently by thirsty Cincinnatians who went there to buy liquor, which was available only at package stores in Ohio. The fact that a quick trip over the river meant one could freely purchase all of the Four Roses one wanted made the Ohio liquor law seem ridiculous.

When "Beale Street" ended, the band took a break, and Norm Hathaway joined Noble. He was quite tall, courtly, and as sliver-thin as sliced bacon. His frequent smile was as open as his sense of humor. His tallness made those around him seem smaller, and Nobel had a tendency to straighten up in his presence. His hair was thick and healthy, and there was little doubt that he would take it all with him to his grave; extreme for the time—long and curling over the neck—it was his musician's badge of artistic independence. Norm was hep. Norm was a cat. Even the way he held his ciga-

Getting Sentimental over You

rette—loosely in his fingers with his hand rolled back—told you he was several miles beyond the ordinary. He was wearing a shawl-collared, powder-blue band jacket, severely draped black trousers, white shirt, and maroon tie. Norm was a sharp, creased, starched, impeccable, "with it" second trumpet player in one of Cincinnati's hottest bands. He was the epitome of cool.

Norm was sympathetic to Noble's story. "Man, that's a drag. But at least she was cool about the tickets. A lot of chicks would expect you to hang around the house and put up with the kid brother and eat leftover chicken." He slid a pack of Raleighs from his pocket, tapped out a cigarette, lit it, blew a long tunnel of smoke. "Hey, besides, it's too nice a day to hang around with some brat. Hell, any day's too nice to hang around with a brat, man. Life's too short. And this way you get to have a few beers and dig Dorsey. A helluva band. Great charts. Sy Oliver. Dorsey gets a great sound. Smooth. Like glass. He's a great musician. He and Teagarden and Miller. All great trombone players. Those cats can play almost anything in first position." He reflected vacantly over his cigarette, rolling it in his fingers. "Hey, who knows, maybe you'll meet somebody else."

"I doubt it."

"You never know, man. I've seen a whole lotta people hook up on this boat. He nodded in the direction of a nice-looking, elderly couple standing nearby. "Like that couple over there. Now there's a real story."

"Oh."

"They met on the first *Queen* back in 1897."

"1897? C'mon."

"Hey, man, the *Island Queen's* been running between Cincy and Coney since '96."

Noble had no idea. "You're kidding?"

"No jive."

"That means they've been riding for—"

"For forty-five years. In fact, they had a big anniversary celebration for 'em earlier this summer right here on the boat. Friends, kids, grandkids, relatives—you name it. A big thing, man. Food. Drinks. They had the boat all decorated up, and everything. It was in all the papers. The band played the gig, so I was here. People got up and talked about 'em. Lots. One helluva story. She was from this poor German family in Price Hill. He was a premed student

Getting Sentimental over You

at UC. His old man was a big-time developer who built half the homes in Hyde Park—Sam Hoffman."

"I've heard of him. They've got this big statue of him on Fifth Street."

"That's the guy. People who give away money love to be bronzed. He donated most of Fountain Square, so I guess they figured they owed him something. They had more money than good sense. It was a real close family. Were very strict Lutherans. She, on the other hand, wasn't real religious and came from a working-class family. Her dad worked at Burger and was on the low rung of the Democratic party. She was going to UC, too, but on a scholarship because she had more brains than Old Man Hoffman had money. Was very smart and independent—big stuff for a girl back then. Socially, the two of 'em were oil and water."

"How'd they ever get together?"

"This is where the *Queen* comes in." He studied his cigarette as though his story were written on it. "She was here with her girlfriends, and he was with a bunch of rich guys from school. You know? Guys with short hair and square suits. Two different parties. Two different worlds. I mean, in those days, people who had bread didn't mingle with people who didn't. Understand? You dig? Remember, this was back in 1897. There was this class thing. But there was one thing that they had in common—they were both good dancers. They lived to dance.

So, the way they tell it, when the music started up and he sees her dancing with one of her girlfriends and sees how good she is, he cuts in. Well . . . I guess they were like Adele and Fred, or something. It was like they'd been partners all their lives. So they danced all the way up the river, all day at Coney, and all the way back on the boat that night. This is how it started. And, even though there was all of this social stuff between them, they fell in love. Well, Old Man Hoffman flipped when the kid told him they were gonna get married. Pulled the rug out from under him, cut him off completely. But this didn't stop him. They went over to Newport and got married that same year. She finished up in political science, and he got his degree in medicine. They raised five kids, she taught school, he became a big-time surgeon. In spite of the differences, their love was stronger than Hyde Park, the Lutheran church, and Old Man Hoffman's dough. Although he finally came around. Grandkids have a way of causing that."

"Wow. That's a neat story."

"Yeah, but that isn't the neatest part." He nodded in their direction again. "Dig how they still look at each other. They're still in love, man, just like when they met. That's what's neat."

And he was right.

They stood close, holding hands, looking out over the river through the glass partition that enclosed the ballroom. Occasionally he would pat her lovingly on the shoulder, and they would share a look of deep caring. She was thin and still remarkably erect in her bearing considering her advanced age. Her gray hair was soft and youthfully styled, not tightly curled as was the hair of most women her age. Her dress was sheer and flowing and feminine. At her neck a silk scarf of pastel hues picked up the essence of her understated makeup. The man wore a Palm Beach suit and—even though it was warm—a shirt and tie. He was immaculate. But not in a starchy way, rather in a manner of cool, relaxed, casual elegance. A boater hat with a black grosgrain band cast an oblique shadow over his handsome features. A prominent, aquiline nose gave him a profile of strong character. They were a distinguished couple. And it was plainly evident they were very much in love.

Noble studied them with great interest, thinking about Norm's story, about how they'd met on the river forty-five years ago. When they exchanged smiles, Noble could sense the warmth, the caring, the bond of mutual respect they shared due to a lifetime of experiences. And when he leaned down and kissed her, it was a long, tender kiss—a youthful kiss. They were still lovers.

Noble thought it remarkable that these people could still be this much in love. Most married people he knew—his aunts and uncles, neighbors, his mother and father—didn't express tenderness. If they were in love, you'd never know it. He wondered if they had ever shared moments of romance and passion and recklessness. If so, it wasn't evident now in their attitudes of polite indifference. Their lives seemed to be loveless, slow-measured beats,

Getting Sentimental over You

dull thuds in a monotonous tempo of living. Even though there was politeness, courtesy, and shows of respect, there were no outward displays of affection, no caresses, no kisses, no gentle touching. Had these people ever been lovers? He thought about this in a deep and reflective way, and his mind flashed to the photograph of his parents on his dresser.

A few random bass notes from the bandstand told Norm that intermission was over. "Well, gotta get back, man. See ya up the river."

CHAPTER SEVEN

NORM returned to the stand and joined the brass section. After charts were sorted, the band swung into "Lover Come Back to Me." The music filled the glass-enclosed deck, swelling it, pushing at it, making it seem bigger. Jitterbuggers, moving with rhythmical four-to-the-bar exuberance, became a kaleidoscope of arms, legs, bobby socks, and saddle shoes. And for a few liberating moments, each couple was lost in musical delirium, off somewhere in another world, a world where they were other than themselves, better than themselves, bigger than themselves, a place where they were romantic and special and carefree. Heads back, eyes de-

Getting Sentimental over You

tached, they spun out and above and beyond their cares and jobs and worries and the boring minutiae of daily responsibility. From the top of the chart, to the coda, to the second ending, till the double bar—during the brief lifetime of "Lover Come Back to Me"—they were in Make Believe Ballroom.

After "Lover Come Back to Me"—when the band shifted down to "Stardust"—the older couple moved to the dance floor and joined others who, like them, weren't up to the "jump" tunes anymore. He guided her gently as they moved smoothly over the floor, holding her as if she were Dresden china. His arm encircled her waist easily, moving her, leading her through the intricacies of the dance. Her white-gloved hand rested easily on his shoulder.

Noble bought another beer and pretzel and went to the top deck to better enjoy the scenic, ten-mile cruise to Coney Island.

Below, lines were cast off and the *Queen* back-paddled from the landing. After retreating a few yards, the engines were reversed and the craft surged slightly as it gained momentum and headed for mid-river. The engine labored as it gained speed, pushing the long, oily shafts that rotated the big paddle wheels. Water boiled from beneath the paddles in agitated trails. Black smoke unfolded from the twin funnels and dissipated into lacy, gray wisps as it rose skyward.

They were under way.

The *Queen* moved up river between Ohio and Kentucky—the top of one, the bottom of the other. On their shores, homes grand and humble stood like sentinels guarding the extremes of the respective states. Even though divided only by the river—an expanse of a few hundred yards—Ohio and Kentucky were different. Not overtly, but in a subtle way. They "felt" different. Whenever Noble crossed the Newport Suspension Bridge into Kentucky, he experienced the sensation of entering a different culture. He couldn't define the feeling, he just knew it felt different. History had dictated this—Ohio was The North; Kentucky, The South. During the days of slavery, Ohio was a sanctuary for blacks, a place of abolitionists and the underground railroad. For them, the state, so near, which bore no significant difference in appearance or climate to Kentucky, represented the Promised Land. The Ohio River was a free-

Getting Sentimental over You

dom river, a flowing, green line dividing blue and gray.

As the *Queen* swam eastward, Cincinnati's skyline was put to rest relentlessly below the city's seven hills. The Broadway landing was long gone, Mt. Adams was falling from view. Behind the boat in canoes, exuberant young men—laughing, bare-chested, bronzed—were attempting to surf her wake. They stayed with the boat until fatigue dictated they abandon their cheery pursuit, finally falling behind with waves and shouts, becoming small, bobbing objects as the Queen paddled steadily away. On either side of the river, the scene grew progressively more rural as large grain-quilts replaced the density of homes, and silos—looking like rockets—stood at protective attention over big farms.

The boat was now mid-river, where the water was deep and rolling and deceptively rapid. Debris—branches, driftwood, various items of flotsam—slid by proudly as if on display. White clouds populated the sky and occasionally moved across the sun, giving the river a dark, viscous quality.

The band was taking intermission and the

calliope was puffing out "Camptown Races." The calliope was programmed to play nothing but songs of the Old South and, one felt, without the melodies of Stephen Foster, its repertoire would have been severely limited. It was a huge affair of multiple pipes and was driven by steam from the *Queen's* boilers. It emitted a powerful, shrill, breathy-voiced sound that gave a circus-like aura to the excursion. But it was a festive sound, in keeping with the trip up the river and the elegant old sidewheeler. Children loved the calliope and stood before it wide eyed as its long, metal pipes expelled octaves of steam.

Noble turned and scanned the crowded upper deck: children, couples, families, GIs up from Bragg and Dix, picnickers with baskets overstuffed with home cooking that would soon overstuff them. He studied the GIs, noting their exuberance, their youth, their attitudes starchy as their khakis. What did the future hold for these smiling men-children on this Ohio River day? He reflected on the headlines and newsreels and small stars suspended in the windows of many Cincinnati homes.

At the stern, three young women were chatting animatedly. They were attractive, in their early twenties. Their clothing had the look of money. It hung differently, draped in a way no cheap material could. Noble noticed this. Being a clothes horse who spent much too much of his salary on wardrobe, their upscale dress, the details—skirts, shoes, jewelry, hair, mannered attitude—did not escape him. He placed his arms over the rail, leaned back, crossed his legs, and observed them approvingly, smiling, slightly bemused. One of the women, as if sensing him there, turned suddenly in his direction. Her voice soared over the calliope: "Noble!"

It was Amy Fox.

CHAPTER EIGHT

HER home was among the nicest in Bond Hill; a three-story Victorian set far back on a quiet street of low-hanging maples and pool-felt lawns. It had deep, sloping eaves that made it look lazy, like it was sleeping. There were ancient trees on the property with huge, exposed roots that reached out errantly like arthritic tentacles. Bond Hill (like the north side) also slept on Sundays and was serenely, almost eerily silent. It was as though it had been cotton-padded for the Sabbath.

Earlier that morning Amy Fox had been in her closet selecting her outfit for the day. It was

Getting Sentimental over You

a walk-in closet, and clothing was hung on three sides. There were built-in drawers for sweaters, lingerie and accessories. At the bottom, on angled racks, shoes were tiered in neat rows.

She stood deep in the closet, surrounded by clothing, arms folded across her chest. She pushed clothing this way and that, sorting through the garments like a shopper at a sale rack. Finally she selected a gathered skirt and a soft-yellow peasant blouse. She spread the skirt on her bed and tucked the blouse into it, forming a shapeless Amy Fox. She stood back, thinking, moving her head from side to side, studying "the look." Was it too dressy? Too casual? The outfit had to be right, she thought, right for the occasion, for the excursion to Coney Island on the *Island Queen*. What she wore was important. She wanted to be part of the crowd but—at the same time—distinctive.

While her radio played "There Are Such Things," she turned and studied herself critically in the full-length mirror on the inside of her closet door. There was little to criticize. Her body was lean. Her legs were long and shapely. The morning sun, entering as big as you please through a leaded-glass panel, fell on her lissome body, abstracting it prismatically. While of average height, she seemed taller because her hair—black and thick—was pinned up attractively over her good features. No one would have ever guessed that she had been considered a "dud" at Hughes High. Gone was the excess weight and the round puffiness from too many Clark bars and double malts. Gone was the plain, unruly hair. Gone were the baggy cardigans and the sensible shoes. Gone forever was the girl who had been about as interesting to boys as used paper. She had, finally, after high school, awakened to the potentials of her exceptional physical qualities. No more Clark bars and malts and old-lady sweaters and Girl Scout shoes and hair as straight as coat-hanger wire. She had seen the light and had made the adjustments, which resulted in the shiny, brand new, 1942 model of Miss Amy Fox. She was in showroom condition.

She slipped into the skirt and blouse and tucked the blouse neatly into the waistband. She cinched a wide belt abound her middle and put on bobby socks and highly shined penny loafers. A quick, once-over turn before the mir-

Getting Sentimental over You

ror sent her skirt spinning. She was satisfied with what she saw. She was ready. A one-piece swimsuit and towel were folded carefully and placed in a small canvas tote. A final item was the addition of a cashmere sweater for the return trip. The summer evenings could be cool on the river.

On the front porch, Sam Fox, a lawyer in one of Cincinnati's most prestigious firms and a highly respected member of the Jewish community, was engrossed in a letter when Amy joined him, diverting him from his reading. He lowered the letter and beamed at her over its pages. He was justifiably proud of his daughter, who had been an honor-roll performer at Hughes High and was now a brilliant fourth-year English Lit major at UC. And she had blossomed. His little girl of once-dowdy appearance and painful reticence was now an attractive, outgoing young woman.

"What time you leaving?"

"Any minute. Beth and Sue are picking me up."

"Big day?"

"Not really. We're just going to hang around Sunlite Pool and ride the rides, and stuff. And have a picnic. Sue's bringing a basket. Letter?"

"From your Uncle Harry. Things are bad over there. Thank God they got into Switzerland in time. They had to leave everything, you know. Everything. Every day it seems to get worse."

"Yes. Awful." She looked up the street in both directions.

"I see where Tommy Dorsey's going to be at Moonlite tonight."

"Yes."

"Are you guys going?"

"No. Beth and Sue have to be home early. Ah! Here they come now."

A yellow Buick convertible ducked to the curb; a Roadmaster with leather seats, a whip of an antenna, its radio full of Frank Sinatra:

> *I'll never smile again*
> *Until I smile at you,*
> *I'll never laugh again*
> *What good would it do . . .*

Amy kissed her father and ran from the porch to the car. He watched her until the Buick disappeared in a slash of yellow around a distant curve. Alone on the porch with the letter carrying the grim news from abroad, he thought about his daughter and the promise she held. This was someone special, someone who would one day be a recognized author and raise a fine Jewish family. Her future was bright. He was fortunate, he thought, to be safe in America with his family, friends, and a daughter who would make any father proud.

CHAPTER NINE

APPROACHING *Noble fast from across the Queen's top deck, Amy Fox presented a picture of a suntanned, elegant young woman. She stood out among the other passengers to the point of aberrance. Her hair, dense and black, shone like liquid ebony in the sun. The cinched, gathered skirt accented the sensual curvature of her body. Men turned as she whisked past, ogling her head to toe.*

Noble hadn't seen her since they had graduated from Hughes High School four years earlier. In school they hadn't been familiar. Or friendly. Or anything, really. They were just a

Getting Sentimental over You

couple of students, detached, passing in hallways or sharing a class. Amy lived in a world of bookish, dowdy friends who were considered "duds" by the kids who were "hep"—the kids who counted. Noble would see her daily in senior English class, but he really never saw her. Instead, his attention was usually riveted upon lovely Audry McClure, whose Angora-sweatered breasts were magnetizing things.

While English had thoroughly escaped Noble, Amy was a brilliant traveler in the land of modifiers, verbs, nouns, predicates, prepositions, and punctuation. She was a serious student and a member of The National Honor Society, the debating team, the Latin Club, the Drama Club (she had once read dryly from Shakespeare's *Sonnets* during assembly), and the Spanish Club. She wrote articles and poetry for the school paper, *The Gargoyle*.

As Amy Fox approached him on this brightly serene Sunday in August, he did his best to sketch in her details. But his recollection of her was vague. At best, he could only remember her as a plain, withdrawn, overweight intellectual, a girl lacking excitement whose pursuits seemed—though admirably lofty—lackluster and boring. She was seldom seen at dances or athletic events or the local hangouts where the popular kids congregated. He remembered her, but in no great detail and with no great distinction. At Hughes High she had been just another face in the crowd. So far as he was concerned—as she approached him on this day—he was meeting a stranger, because this was certainly not the Amy Fox he had known. Not this tanned thoroughbred who was quickly closing in.

But Amy remembered Noble Johnson. Remembered him well. He was easy to remember. How could she forget one of the most popular boys in school? How could she forget someone who had lettered in football, basketball, and track? How could she possibly forget this tall, handsome jock who rolled gently when he walked? She couldn't. And didn't.

During their four years at Hughes, Noble had been highly conspicuous. Not only for his good looks, and his presence on the playing field and in the gym, but for his ubiquitous presence on campus. He had been as enormously popular as she hadn't been, seemingly always surrounded by friends or in the pres-

Getting Sentimental over You

ence of the prettiest girls in school—especially Audry McClure, whom, she recalled, was with him exclusively during their senior year. She saw him often, moving athletically through the halls, always surrounded by admirers because he was a gregarious person of great charm. Often, after school, she'd see him on the front steps of the building surrounded by friends or climbing into a car to be accelerated from the curb in a burst of exhaust and laughter.

She admired him, but also resented him and others like him for possessing traits impossible for her—easiness in the company of others, relaxed conversation, an apparent lack of self-consciousness around those of the opposite sex. She had been envious of anyone having these easy social ways. It hurt her deep down to see other girls her age—frivolous, poor students—float so effortlessly on the social sea. So she hid in her books and behind her intellect, peeking out with resentment upon the world of relaxed intercourse—the world of Noble Johnson. But she couldn't ignore him. What girl could? Although she was overweight, bookish, and shy, she was still a young woman with a young woman's urges and desires. But, during her teen years, she just couldn't let go, free herself from her self-doubts and insecurities. She lived within herself, wound down tight inside her self-protective shell. It was unnecessarily, because there was a whole lot more to Amy Fox than met the eye. Amy Fox was a package waiting to be unwrapped.

She took his hand firmly. There was no sign of shyness, nor self-doubt, nor trace of the old uneasiness. She was direct and available. Her intelligent, brown eyes looked up at him intently, sincerely. It was as if (even though they'd had virtually no contact during high school) she was greeting an old friend. "I'm Amy Fox. Amy Fox. Remember? Senior English? Miss Rauch's English class?"

He'd been caught off guard, and his attempt to cover was clumsy. "Oh, yeah. Yeah. Sure. Amy Fox. Of course."

"You didn't remember me at all, did you?"

"At first, I didn't. I gotta admit."

" I could have been anyone."

"Well, it's been a while, you know."

"Four years."

"We both had Miss Rauch?" He looked down at her, finding it hard to believe that this

Getting Sentimental over You

was the same Amy Fox that had sat three rows over near the window.

"I hated that class."

"You? If I remember, you had English down cold."

He was as she had remembered him. Tall. Trim. Well-dressed. And he hadn't aged. He just seemed to be an older teen. "You haven't changed a bit, you know that?"

"Well . . . maybe. But I can't say the same for you. You look great. Different. No wonder I didn't recognize you at first." This was an understatement. He couldn't believe the transformation. He thought back, putting himself inside the stuffy confines of Miss Rauch's classroom, where the wall clock ticked, its slow pendulum swings slicing eternity into seconds. The dry odor of chalk. The squeak of the warped wooden floors as students went to the board to diagram a sentence or delineate some (at least to him) abstruse literary proposition.

He compared the images—the old classroom Amy and the *Island Queen* Amy. There was no comparison. The change was stark. Pleasantly so. It was as though she had jumped from grainy black and white to Technicolor.

"I got fed up with being plain and oveweight." She looked anything but now. There, in the Ohio River sun, on the upper deck of the *Queen*, looking up at over six feet of Noble, she was a stunner. Realizing that she was still clutching his hand, she pulled it away quickly. "I was such a klutz during high school. I was looking through the Hughes Annual the other day. I looked like the Old Dutch Cleanser Woman. No wonder you never noticed me."

"Well . . ." He fumbled for a second. He couldn't have agreed more, but propriety reigned. "I remember you as being real smart. You always seemed to have the answers to everything."

"Not really. If I'd had the answers, you'd remember me for more than just being smart." She looked him over with admiration. He had taken care of himself. Even though it had only been four years since high school, many of her former classmates had become adults too quickly, gaining weight, already slipping toward a premature middle age. But not Noble Johnson. He was still as she remembered him, sliding down the hallways of Hughes High in his letter sweater—handsome, boyish, at com-

Getting Sentimental over You

plete ease in his skin. He was still the same boyish, masculine, handsome student she had slyly eyed across the city of desks in senior English. "What have you been doing with yourself?"

"Not much. Working out at Chevy. Waiting for the man with the top hat and beard to point his finger. 'Noble Johnson, I want you.'"

"Yes, the war. Terrible."

"I'd planned on going to college on a football scholarship. I was all-city at Hughes."

"All everything, you mean." This was her recollection of him. The Golden Boy. The guy on the Wheaties box.

"Except in the books department. I had a heck of a time keeping up. Anyway, I had some colleges scout me, and I figured I was all set. Then, during the last season at Hughes, I dislocated both of my shoulders during the Woodward game." He bit his lip and looked off. He rolled his shoulders forward as if testing them. The memory lingered. "That pretty much did it so far as college was concerned. I'd never have gotten in on my grades, that's for sure. After graduation, that summer, I kinda bounced around.

"I played a lot of sports, and drank way too much beer at Mecklenberg Gardens and Crosley Field. I don't think I missed a single Reds home game. It was a good summer. No responsibility. And I was still living at home, so it didn't put too much of a strain on my pocketbook. And I spent a lot of time up here—at Coney Island, that is. I lived up here during that summer, messing around, swimming, dancing at Moonlite. Great place, Moonlite.

"That winter I got a job as a sub mail carrier. Figured I had to do something to raise money for Christmas and to keep up my end at Mecklenberg's. Wasn't too bad a job, although my feet got awful cold making the second loop.

"Then I gave life insurance a try. Western Southern. But after a few weeks, I decided selling death for a living wasn't my game. Next I got a job in the women's shoe department at McAlpin's. It was a good job, and I got to dress up every day. I was their leading salesman, and I made some nice bonuses. It was easy. A snap, really. All you had to do was tell a woman she was a size 5AAA, even though she measured 7B. In shoe sales, flattery will get you everywhere. But, after a while, I got tired of handling

Getting Sentimental over You

feet and lying for a buck.

"Then, when this job opened up at Chevy—my Uncle Richard got me in—I jumped at it. I do okay. I've got my own place now and enough money to blow on good times and clothes and such. That's about it, I guess."

The calliope had ceased its shrill, wheezy, program and the band was once again playing. He studied her intently, still amazed by her transformation. "Okay, your turn. How about you? You working?"

"No. I'm still at school. At UC."

"Ah, a coed."

"Yes. Is that bad?"

"No, no. Not at all. It's good. Besides, it's you."

"I hope that's a compliment."

"It is. I mean, you were always college. You had college written all over you. No doubt about it. With your grades?" He studied her and there was quiet between them for a few seconds. Then: "Where you living?"

"I'm still at home. In Bond Hill." She felt odd about this. It was as if she were confessing to lingering adolescence, an inability to be on her own. She hurried to explain. "I'd get my own place, but it really doesn't make much sense while I'm going to UC. Besides, I don't think the dorm life's for me. And my mother passed away last year, so I don't want to leave my father right now. He's still in shock. He just can't seem to get over it."

"Gee. I'm sorry."

"It was totally unexpected. Are you married?"

"Me?" He was amused by her question. "God, no."

Hadn't married? She couldn't believe it. How could he have escaped?

"Anyway, there's no hurry. And with the war.... What about you?"

"I'm afraid not."

"Really? Someone who looks like you?"

She wouldn't have heard this a few years earlier. It was a huge compliment. Especially coming from this tall, Bay-Rumed, good-looking man who had hardly known she'd existed at Hughes High. "It's not in my plans. I mean, with school and all."

"Then, you went right into college?"

"Right. That fall. During the summer I was pretty much a stay-at-home. Did a lot of reading. It was my way of avoiding the fact that I was unpopular, I guess. So I lived inside of books—fantasized. I remember how I would have died to have been Daisy in *The Great Gatsby*.

"I fancied myself this intellectual who knew more than anybody else. What it really was, was that I was ashamed of my weight, and for that reason I avoided people—especially boys. I only dated a few times in high school. Billy Creamer. Remember him?"

"Yeah, I think so. Wasn't he the skinny kid with the thick glasses who looked like he was in pain all the time?"

She laughed at the accuracy of his description. "That's him. He was even more bookish than I was. Anyway, that's kind of the way it went till about mid-way through my sophomore year. Then, one day while I was at Pogue's trying to squeeze my size fourteen body into an eight, I decided enough was enough. I'd had it. So I went on a diet of no Clark bars and less intellect and started exercising. With getting thinner and working at not being a bore came more dates and a heck of a lot more fun. Looking back now. . ." she shuddered at the recollection, "ugh—I was a mess."

"Well, you sure aren't now. You look sensational." Noble nodded in the direction of Amy's companions on the rear deck. "Friends?"

"Yes. From college."

"Then, you don't have a date?"

"No. We decided it'd be more fun going by ourselves. Kind of a relief now and then, you know. What about you?"

"I did have, but something came up. With Audry McClure, as a matter of fact. You remember her?"

"Audry McClure? Miss Angora Sweaters? How could I forget Audry McClure? How could anyone?"

"She still looks good."

"I'll bet. I'm sure of it. Are you two . . . ? I mean . . . " She tensed her mouth in reaction to a question that may have been too personal. "Sorry."

"That's okay. No, we're just good friends. Have been since Hughes. We go out a lot. Dancing, mostly. She's a great dancer." He quickly shifted the subject away from Audry. "Lemme ask you: Are you still the smartest girl in Cincy?"

Getting Sentimental over You

"I never was. What ever gave you that idea?"

"C'mon. You were a brain."

She accordioned her nose at this. "I never liked that term. It always made me sound like some kind of freak, or something."

"Hey. It's nothing to be ashamed of."

"It just the image that goes with it, that's all. 'Brain.' 'Know-it-all.' Those terms kind of pigeonhole you, you know."

He looked at her admiringly. "Well, I'd pigeonhole you as a real attractive woman."

She reddened a bit, looking down at her loafers, experiencing a warming inner surge. She had received the compliment before, but it hadn't had the same impact. This time she felt it. It was the way he'd said it. Softly. Sincerely. There was nothing unctuous in his remark, nothing that could be construed as a "line," nothing in it that would indicate that it was in any way calculated to gain advantage. It was just a straightforward, genuine observation. It was typical of him, she thought, thinking back. This was the quality she had sensed about him at Hughes—his obvious sincerity. He had always (even in view of his great popularity) seemed to be someone without guile or underlying motive, someone who was honest and real. Attractive woman. Attractive woman. His remark echoed inside her head. Yes, she had heard this often before. But this was the first time it had made her feel as though she really were.

Small talk and pleasant laughter took them around the long sweep of River Bend and into the final stretch before Coney Island. They conversed like old friends after a long separation, comfortable in each other's presence, intently absorbed, slipping deeper and deeper into each other with every word. The casual observer would have been surprised to learn that they had never spoken a word previously, that the only connection they shared was class photos bound between the slick pages of the Hughes yearbook. They appeared to be old friends recalling the intimacies of a lifetime of experiences. Their talk was the kind that was engrossing, the kind that cut out the world and stopped the clock and placed them far beyond the moment.

Below, the river churned under the paddle wheels. In the ballroom, the sound of "My Rev-

Getting Sentimental over You

erie" escaped its glass confines and swam on the river. Children ran and shouted playfully, ignoring the weak pleas of inattentive mothers. The sound of a thousand passengers—muted and loud and in between—ebbed and flowed around them. But they were oblivious. These things didn't exist in the vacuum of their absorption. Noble and Amy on this day, at this moment, were on more than a Sunday excursion up the Ohio, they were on a voyage around themselves. They talked. And talked. And, as the boat pulled Coney Island slowly nearer, they discovered each other there in the river sunlight of that long-ago August day.

The high-pitched, excited voice of a child blended with the boat's throaty whistle, shattering their concentration: "Hey, Mom! There's Coney!"

From the top deck of the *Queen*, Amy and Noble could see Rivergate, the wharf where the *Island Queen* moored and disgorged its passengers. From the wharf, a wide path wound upward. A few hundred feet up the path stood the Coney Island Lighthouse. It was a symbol of welcome and a landmark for the traffic—barges and pleasure boats—that moved up and down the Ohio. At night, its light fingered out over the river in long sweeps, caressing the water and flashing the homes on the Kentucky shore. Beyond the lighthouse, the path disappeared into a thickly wooded grove and meandered to Coney's main gates where—after purchasing tickets—people were spun through turnstiles into the park itself. In the far distance, above the trees, they could see a car creep to the top of the wooden framework of the Wild Cat roller coaster and drop silently, suddenly from view.

Amy gently pushed back errant tendrils of hair blowing about her face. "You come here often?" she asked.

"Every now and then. Almost always when a name band's playing. How about you?"

"Oh, maybe a couple of times a summer. I have since I was a kid. It's kind of a tradition."

"Are you guys going to stay for Dorsey?"

"No."

"You're kidding?"

"Beth and Sue," she indicated in their direction, "the girls I came with—they have to be back early. We're just going to ride some rides. Swim. Have a picnic."

Getting Sentimental over You

"Gee, that's too bad. Nobody should miss Dorsey. The last time he was here, he set a record—almost 4,500 people. That's when he had Sinatra with him."

The boat eased into Rivergate and was secured. Its forward ramp was lowered. People surged over the ramp and up the walkway, past the lighthouse and into the woods, Noble and Amy and her friends among them. The woods were dense and cool. Along the path were picnic tables and recreation facilities. Tents had been erected to house some of the tables. People—families and groups—were breaking off and staking out tables and areas that would be theirs for the day. Amy's friends, carrying food-laden wicker baskets, walked awkwardly with their loads. Seeing this, Noble relieved them of the baskets, taking them without effort as if they were lighter than air.

Well into the grove, the girls spotted a picnic table a few feet from the path. It was of heavy oak and covered with initials and inscriptions that had been carved deeply into the wood. Its seats were smooth and had a soft patina from many seasons of use. After Noble had placed the baskets on the table, the girls unfolded a checkered tablecloth and spread it neatly over the table, carefully smoothing out wrinkles with their hands. Then they began to unpack the dinnerware and food.

"Will you join us for lunch?" Amy asked.

"No. I don't think so."

"Oh, c'mon." There was encouragement from her friends as well.

"No thanks."

"We have plenty, more than enough."

"I'm really not very hungry."

She was peeling back wax paper from a plate of fried chicken. "We'll never eat all of this food."

"I had too many pretzels on the boat." They persisted, but he was firm in his rejection. "I couldn't eat a thing. Really. You guys go ahead. You're going swimming later, aren't you?"

"Yes."

"Well then . . . I'll see you at the pool." He backed away graciously, smiling, putting distance between himself and their pleas for him to remain.

They watched him as he moved away over the picnic grounds, gracefully weaving among the tables, skillfully dodging the occasional darting child. Tall and well-groomed, he stood

Getting Sentimental over You

out in bold contrast to his surroundings, his presence bringing a touch of elegance to the scene. The girls remarked about this and questioned Amy about him. Their natural, feminine curiosity had been aroused. They wanted to know about this good-looking young man. She told them all she knew, what she remembered about him from Hughes High, of his great popularity and athletic ability, and they were greatly impressed. As was she. This was evident in her eyes as she watched him until he was absorbed by a distant crowd.

CHAPTER TEN

HE had wanted to picnic with Amy and her friends, but his mannerly nature dictated that this would have been an intrusion, a disruptive element to a long-planned outing. He thought about this and thought about Amy as he purchased his ticket at Coney's main gate. He recalled their conversation on the Island Queen. Every word. He could remember the total experience in great detail, could project it with his inner eye and view it as if watching actors on a screen. He could picture it all clearly. Her smile. Dress. The warm breeze pushing at her hair. Her face back-lit against the sky. And he saw

Getting Sentimental over You

himself as well, vividly, as a key player in the scene. It was a strange and unusual thing. Amy had touched something in him, something down deep, something that hadn't been touched before. It was at once a disturbing and pleasant feeling. And inexplicable. In an instant, out of nowhere, on this Sunday that had begun as so many before, his life had been irrevocably affected in some profound and moving way. How? Why? These were questions to which Noble Johnson—the casual, carefree young man whose thoughts were of little else than music and new clothes—had no immediate answers. Elated, melancholy, confused, he spun his way through the shiny arms of the turnstile into that Coney Island day. Amy, too, was melancholy. As she helped herself to cold fried chicken and scooped potato salad to her plate, she did so absentmindedly, for her thoughts were elsewhere and muddled. She tried—with her great intelligence—to frame them, put them in perspective, but for once her intelligence failed her. Logic fell away. She had always been able to confront feelings rationally by applying rules and big words and proven methods of clear reasoning. But not this time.

This time the rules and big words and "proven" methods were overpowered by bigger, inexplicable sensations.

Her thoughts were confused by her feelings for the tall fellow with the deep tan and courtly manner she had approached innocently, out of a spirit of camaraderie for high school days. It had been nothing more than an impulse of recognition, an act of social curiosity. She had expected nothing. A nod. A formal handshake. Remember me? How are you? How've you been? A brief update and a swift farewell. But fate had intended otherwise, and all of the rules and all of the intellect and all of the reasoning and all the king's horses and all the king's men wouldn't have been enough to win the battle against the overwhelming odds of her deep feelings. So the chicken was tasteless and the potato salad bland. She was savoring something other than food. Something exotic and rare and disruptive. She didn't know exactly what it was, but it sure tasted good.

It was hot on the midway, so Noble removed his loafer jacket, folded it carefully (wrinkles were out of the question), and slung it over his shoulder. He squinted at the sun, his hand over

Getting Sentimental over You

his eyes in a sort of reverse salute as a shield against it. The sounds of the park—the barkers, carousel, the arcade's tinny music, the mechanical hum of rides—blended to form a muted din around him. He looked down the mall's long expanse. It was wide and paved and clean and had been turned into a boulevard by the symmetrical placement of rectangular islands. The islands had been arranged to create pathways, and each was ringed by low hedges and planted with shrubs, flowers, tightly pruned trees, and other local greenery. The islands ran the length of the mall, acting as conduits for customers while separating the rides and concessions on either side. At the far end, the chalk-white, intricately constructed cross-members of the Wild Cat roller coaster gave it the look of a looming, prehistoric skeleton. Colorful pennants fluttered from poles ringing its uppermost section and long, people-filled cars were being pulled to the top of the steep incline leading to its first dip, where they hovered briefly before slithering down in a rush of clattering screams.

Noble purchased a cone heaped with Creamy Whip, a confection that was soft, velvety, and deliciously vanilla. It also tended to melt rapidly, so Noble held the cone away protectively, licking its sides frequently to keep the ice cream from spotting his spotless powder-blue gabardines. He walked the mall slowly, absorbing with interest its sights and sounds. There was no hurry. None at all. A long, easy day lay ahead before Moonlite opened and the band began to play.

At the Milk Bottle Toss, he stopped to watch sleeve-rolled men attempt the impossible task of triumphing over unfairly weighted bottles. Step right up! Knock 'em down! Three balls for a dime! Bottles were toppled and knocked askew, but none were cleaned from the low platforms as required. So the men would try again and fail again, and the cheap, plaster, Kewpie Doll prizes remained safely glitter-eyed on their shelves. At the Test of Strength, he watched as determined men removed coats with flourishes of purpose and handed them to admiring women. They spat on their hands and rubbed them together dramatically before taking the big wooden mallet and raising it in a long arc above their heads. Then, with a grunt, they swung it mightily to the pad, where it landed with a rubbery thud, propelling the metal weight upward: 50, 60, 70 . . . sometimes past 90 it rose. Once in a while it rang the bell.

In the arcade, the clanks and rattles, the click of machines, their mechanical, metallic smell, reminded Noble of the assembly line at Chevy. Here he found people testing their grips, testing their skills, testing their abilities to beat the games. Men, imagining themselves Joe Louis, slammed their fists to punching bags with frightening energy, causing the bag to slam into the machine's glass and register the "Power of Your Punch." Children, crouched and concentrated to the point of oblivion, carefully manipulated caged claws until they smiled precisely over the enticing prizes below—a pocket knife, an actual Hamilton wrist watch. Easy. Easy. Easy now. Easy. Lower. Lower. Now! They would release the claws, which dropped in flashes of menacing chrome, invariably sliding to the side of the ever-elusive prize. The children would grimace in defeat and look to their parents with agonized, pleading faces. Another nickel, please.

Noble entered the building housing the carousel and took a seat on one of the benches lining its walls. The brightly painted horses were motionless, riderless, at rest. Their overly reddened mouths and intense, wild, wooden eyes gave them the appearance of being angry for their lives of eternal, boring rotation. Hooves raised, they looked as though they were intent on breaking from their highly polished, brass center poles and galloping off to freedom. Rococo filigrees and gold cherubs in full-winged flight decorated the carousel, giving it an alluring cheapness. After purchasing tickets, people poured in and mounted the horses or seated themselves in the sleighs. When the ride was sufficiently loaded, the operator leaned forward on his lever, and the great, colorful top began to spin, slowly gaining momentum as its nickelodeon drummed out a robotic, clangy, midway symphony.

After watching the carousel to the point of vertigo, Noble left the building and bought a chili dog from a vendor on the mall. He found a bench and sat, people-watching as he ate. After finishing his snack, he walked the mall, stopping occasionally to watch the people enjoy the rides. They rode the wild rides with screams of fearful joy and the tame rides with bursts of

Getting Sentimental over You

shrill laughter and emerged from the Laugh-in-the-Dark with eyes of blind bewilderment. They were having fun and were involved and, for a few Sunday hours, removed from the workaday grind and ordinariness of human repetition. Noble seldom cruised the park these days, because he usually arrived later in the company of Audry McClure or some other light-footed young thing for the purpose of hearing the bands and the music and dancing under the stars at Moonlite. But this day was different. He had plenty of time to take in Coney in all of her happy glory. So he made a leisurely tour, a complete circle of the mall, ending up at the Dodge'em attraction, where people were relieving their aggressions by slamming their cars into others with neck-whipping force as cables above spat electricity in bright, spasmodic, hissing bursts.

It was by now well into the afternoon.

Sunlite pool no longer held much attraction for Noble. Not like it had when he was younger and more aggressive and eager to impress the girls with his perfectly executed dives. But today was different. Today Sunlite held a definite attraction. A feature attraction, as a matter of fact—Amy Fox. So Noble wandered the fence ringing the pool, looking for her. (Sunlite was a very big pool. In fact, at 201 x 400 feet, holding 3,000,000 gallons of water, it had the distinction of being one of the largest recirculating swimming pools in the world. It has its own artesian-well pumping system. It had its own filtration plant. It even had its own laundry. And inside the fence that enclosed it there was shuffleboard, table tennis, volleyball, and badminton. There was also a large sand beach and sunbathing area.) Sunlite Pool had everything. And best of all, on this August day, it had Amy Fox.

Noble spotted her sitting on a towel in the sand.

Her body was compact and muscular and tanned and provocatively accentuated by the clinging wetness of her maillot. Her hair had been tucked up under a white-rubber bathing cap, giving her the look of fine statuary. She stood, laughing, pointing off at something of interest across the pool. While there was a casualness to her movements, an off-handed elegance to them that projected relaxed self-control, there was an element of vitality about them, a presence of energy that told you that her self-control would not be taken to the point of self-denial. There in the sand, pointing off, elegant and poised, there was no trace of the Amy Fox of yesterday, the girl in senior English, the dour, withdrawn intellectual. Today she was a woman.

The pool's bathhouse—long and rambling and musty from the smell of wetness—was busy with swimmers padding about on careful feet. At its entrance was a high counter where you could purchase admissions, rent swimwear, and be issued baskets for the storage of street clothes. Here Noble rented swim trunks. They were black and had a wide, white, web belt with a nickel-plated buckle. He was given a wire basket, a towel, and a large-numbered safety-pin. He took the basket to the men's dressing area, where he placed it on a low bench. He removed his clothing and valuables and placed them neatly in the basket, excising great care with the loafer jacket, which he folded professionally (inside out, armhole in armhole) like coats are folded when you buy them at a store. He slipped into the trunks and snapped their nickel-plated buckle. He pinned the numbered pin at an angle through the trunks and checked it to make sure it was securely fastened. It was.

Returning his basket to one of the attendants at the front counter, Noble said, "Be sure you take good care of this, okay?"

The attendant was used to handling hundreds of these baskets each day, so his reply was cursory at best. Perhaps a bit flip. "Sure, bud."

"Sure, what?" Here came the serious side of Noble Johnson. The loafer jacket not only represented many hours of overtime, it was also the best from the rack of 44 longs at Pogue's Department Store.

The attendant was vastly unconcerned. "I said, sure. Whatever you say, sure," he said, shoving Noble's basket recklessly into a bin.

Noble leaned in over the counter. "Excuse me." When the attendant turned back, he found Noble's wide shoulders spreading above him. "What's your name, kid?"

The attendant, looking up at the expanse of muscle and bone, answered in a thin, nervous vibrato. "Jerry, sir."

Noble leaned in further. His presence was

Getting Sentimental over You

powerful and dominating. "Well, Jerry . . . " He paused before adding, with a nod at the basket, in a deep, cool, resonant voice, "I'd sure hate to see anything happen to that jacket."

The boy's answer was forced and feeble and chuckled, but there wasn't any humor in it. "Oh. Oh sure. Okay. You bet. I understand. Gotcha." He pulled Noble's basket from the collection of others that formed a mountain of wire behind him, handling it carefully, beaming with a smile of oily accommodation. I'll keep it right under here. Right here under the counter. Okay? Just ask for me."

"I will. Jerry, right?"

"Yes, sir."

This is where Noble's smile (an effective, disarming tool) came in handy. It spread wide and white at Jerry, removing all traces of the menacing innuendo that had preceded it. "Thanks, Jerry. I knew I could depend on you." He flipped the boy a small, quick salute, turned, and exited, his broad back silhouetted in the doorway leading to the pool. He was content, satisfied, confident that his loafer jacket was now as safe as if it were in the vault at Fifth Third Bank.

CHAPTER ELEVEN

AMY *saw Noble the moment he stepped from the bathhouse. He would have been hard to miss. His athletic carriage, his muscular physique, placed him in another dimension from the other swimmers. She watched him as he approached, moving among the crowd gracefully, stepping through the sand with easy rotations of his feet. Until he stood above her.*

"I'm not interrupting anything, am I?"

"No."

"I mean . . . you're here with your friends. I don't wanna be a problem."

She pointed to her friends, who were sitting across the pool talking with two deeply tanned young men. "It looks like I'm the last thing on their minds."

Noble seated himself beside her, drew his legs up, and rested his forearms on his knees. He squinted out over the pool. "I'm surprised you're not over there with them."

"Why should I be over there? I was waiting for you."

He looked at her. Her eyes were as direct as her statement. He was both surprised and pleased that she was so straightforward. "You're kidding?"

"You said, 'I'll see you at the pool.' Remember?"

"Sure, I know, but—"

"So, I've been waiting. It wouldn't be very nice of me to be sitting here with some beach boy, now, would it?" And it wouldn't have suited her plans anyway. She was looking forward to seeing him again, talking with him, exploring further the feelings he had stirred in her.

"Well, I'm glad."

"Me, too."

He studied her. She was lovely. Not in a pretty or demure or delicate way, but rather in a way that took her well beyond the boundaries of ordinary beauty. There was so much about her that attracted him: the easy, subtle gestures; the way she pouted her mouth when thinking; the slight cock of her head when she listened; the eyes that saw only you; the voice that was warm as a good cello that kind of surrounded you with its resonating softness. "I just can't believe how much you changed."

She closed her eyes, tilted her head back, and directed her remark to the sun. "It was about time. I was a mess, wasn't I?"

"A mess? No, no. Of course not. You were just—different, I mean, just kind of— "

She interrupted his obviously defensive reply. "A mess. If you don't believe me, take a good look at my class photo sometime. God. I look like something right out of Bleak House. On second thought, don't look."

"Hey, c'mon, everybody looks dopey in those pictures."

"Not you. You were gorgeous. And still are."

He wasn't comfortable with this. Her flattery left him feeling awkward and big and conspicuous. It wasn't that he was unaware of being handsome, he wasn't, but it had never mattered to him to any great extent. He passed over her comment. "So you're at UC, huh? What's you're major?"

"English Lit."

"Then what?"

"Then I write the Great American Novel, get famous, move to Europe, and become the biggest snob in literary history." She paused momentarily, looking off vacantly, attempting vainly to bring her future into perspective. "I don't know. Not really. Teach, probably. I like working with kids."

"You'd be good with them."

"You think so?"

"Yes."

"You don't even know me."

"You know, for some reason, I feel like I do." This was sincere. Her honesty (her "I was waiting for you") made him feel like he'd known her a long time. I was waiting for you. How many women would have said this, would have been this open and direct? None he'd ever met. Most would have played it aloof, pretending to be coolly indifferent to his arrival. After all, wasn't this the feminine way? But she was better than this, and it made her special.

He continued: "When you walked up to me on the boat today, it was like, like it was right, you know. For you to be there at that moment, I mean. For us to meet like that. For us to be together." He hesitated. "You probably think I'm crazy."

She didn't think anything of the sort. She was impressed by his sensitivity, the poetry of his remarks. It was something she hadn't expected of him. Anyway, she felt the same way. "It was just a crazy impulse. I remembered you from class, and I just figured, 'What the heck.' Besides, you always interested me."

"Really?"

"Because you represented everything I wasn't. Popular. Involved. You always seemed to be so at ease with yourself. Me? I was always balled up inside. Tight and insecure. In fact, I think I secretly resented you—anyone like you—for being so confident and relaxed around people." She paused again, digging her toe into the sand thoughtfully. "And I know what you mean. About how you felt when we met on the boat, that is. You're right. It just seemed perfect, somehow. It was as though it had all been arranged." She pulled the bathing cap from her head, releasing its dark treasure. She snapped her head quickly, and her hair whipped outward before settling into thick, black, lucent folds.

In the large area inside the high fence that enclosed the pool, the flag on the high standard stood out patriotically in the breeze. The floodlights on the tall, thin, metal poles looked down with indifferent, glassy eyes on the noisy swimmers below. The blue-green water was a rippling mirror under the swimmers, reflecting their movements on its surface. Across the pool, Amy's friends chatted with the tanned young men, charming them with contrived laughter, subtle movements, and their womanly mystique. Artie Shaw made an appearance from the cones of large speakers, spreading "What is This Thing Called Love" over the pool, his clarinet's distinctive voice—complemented by a slick arrangement—polishing the melody. It was a special summer moment, immediate and real, but, at the same time, melancholy and far away.

"I think I'll go for a swim." Noble rose and

moved away over the sand. He walked the border of the pool until he'd reached the pool's deep end, the end where the diving boards were. He climbed the tower to the high board and waited his turn in line as others plunged awkwardly from the platform. When it was his turn, he moved to the end of the board. Amy watched. His body was lean and long and hard and, as he raised himself on tiptoes, the muscles of his calves flexed to reverse Ws. As he bent slightly before taking off, his muscles tightened in bold relief, standing out anatomically under his sun-browned skin. Others, as well as Amy, sensed something special and, looking upward, they watched as he prepared to dive. He crouched, then he swung his arms upward in a long arc as he sprung simultaneously from the board. The momentum he'd generated propelled him high above the board, where he rose to an apogee of momentary suspension, seemingly weightless at the top of his flight. Then, birdlike, he spread his arms and dropped gracefully downward, bringing his arms together in front of him a split second before hitting the water, splitting its surface soundlessly, without disturbing it, as though it had

Getting Sentimental over You

been ordered to part for his entrance.

Amy stood as he returned, smiling, applauding softly. "That was something."

"Well, I haven't lost too much, I guess."

"It was beautiful."

"It's been a while."

"You'd never know it."

He went about toweling himself off. "I come out mostly for the bands. For the dancing."

"Not one of my strong suits, I'm afraid."

"Maybe you never had the right partner."

"I have a feeling even Fred Astaire would have trouble with me."

"I doubt it. Not at Moonlite. Moonlite brings out the best."

"I've never been there."

He was astonished. "No!"

"Never."

"You're kidding."

"I swear." She crossed her heart like children do.

"You mean to tell me you've lived here all your life and haven't been to Moonlite?"

"I've always felt like such a klutz when it comes to dancing. Awkward, you know."

He spread his towel and seated himself on it

and she sat, too. "We'll, that's going to change."

She looked at him, cocking her head in the way that attracted him so. "Oh, really?"

"Tonight you're going to Moonlite."

"What are you talking about?"

"Tonight you're going with me to Moonlite Gardens."

"Please."

"It's an order."

"I can't."

"Why can't you?"

"Because we're going home early. Beth and Sue have to be back. And Sue's driving."

He took her hands. She didn't resist. "Look, I've got two tickets to Dorsey, all right? Two hard-to-get tickets to the greatest dance band in America, okay? And what's the point using them just to stand around without dancing?"

"But, I told you, I'm not a good dancer."

"But I don't care. And, besides, that isn't the point."

"Oh, really? What is?"

"The point is, we'll be together."

His point was well taken. As were his points of logic for her staying for dinner and dancing and taking the last boat back to Cincinnati, after which he would drive her to her nice home in Bond Hill. His argument was logical, practical, convincing, and easy to win—because she was in complete agreement.

> *What is this thing called love,*
> *This crazy thing called love . . .*

CHAPTER TWELVE

As the sun began to wear itself out in the west, and coolness settled over the late afternoon, people gathered their things and vacated the pool like an army in chilled defeat. Noble, Amy, and her friends, however, sat in a small circle, talking, laughing, enjoying the remains of the day, until the sun had exhausted itself beyond the woods. Then they gathered their things and headed for the bathhouse.

Jerry returned Noble's basket promptly, pulling if from beneath the counter with officious care and handing it to Noble with an attitude of conciliation. The loafer jacket was neatly folded as Noble had placed it, safe and secure and unwrinkled atop the rest of his clothing. Noble dressed unhurriedly, putting himself back together with care and precision. When he was clothed, he attended to his hair, combing it precisely, parting it in a thin, sharp line.

In the women's dressing area, Amy and her friends discussed the events of the day, the focal point of which was, of course, the tall, handsome man who had unexpectedly come into her life. They gossiped as young women do, her friends expressing friendly envy for her good fortune of Noble, Tommy Dorsey, and Moonlite. It was the thing of which romantic fantasies were made, and they chided her suggestively about the dangers inherent in the intoxicating cocktail of moonlight and music. It was all in good fun and Amy accepted it as intended, as harmless, good-natured, feminine banter.

They all met outside the bathhouse. They were fresh, young, and sunburned—all hope and future. They walked slowly back to the amusement area and for a long time stood talking near the Ferris wheel till it was dusk, the girls not wanting to leave but knowing they must. The Ferris wheel—colorful and intricate—spun above them, turning rocking gondolas in a circle to nowhere. Finally the girls hugged and said goodbye and Noble shook their hands. Then they turned off into the crowd, waving back over it till Noble and Amy could see only their fingertips fluttering in sinking descent over the bobbing heads of people.

The park, although not as crowded as it had been during the shank of the day, was still alive and busy, still catering to the enjoyment of its visitors. There were long lines in front of the Tumble Bug and The Moon Rocket, and the arcade was still ingesting coins. When Noble took Amy's hand, she looked up at him with a compliant smile, a smile that said, I'm glad you did that.

As they walked hand-in-hand down the island-divided midway, the park's lights sputtered to life in rapid succession and suddenly, as if rising from a dream, Coney Island was new and lustrous and spectacular. It suddenly became Broadway, but Broadway in motion, because the rides, electrically outlined,

Getting Sentimental over You

were rotating, undulating, brilliant smears of illumination. The park, by day a colorful gallery of sights and sounds, had been transformed into an exciting, electrified, moving carnival.

Even though it was still crowded, the park became quieter because it was growing dark, and darkness had a way of saying shh. The voices of the carousel nickelodeon, the roller coaster chain, and the hurdy-gurdy were now strangely muted, seemingly speaking softly out of respect for the night. And with the closing darkness came an aura of romance that was enhanced by a recording by Duke Ellington, who—in a sentimental mood—loved it all madly.

On the midway there was a small, unpretentious place to eat with chairs with bentwood backs and small tables covered with red-and-white checkered oilcloths. It was self-service, and its menu board of white-plastic letters—Ms replacing run-out-of Ws—offered such all-American favorites as hot dogs, hamburgers, chili dogs, corn dogs, French fries, plus the Cincinnati standards of bratwurst and beer. Noble ordered bratwursts and beers and took them to the table and then went to a jukebox and made a selection. Harry James proclaimed "You Made Me Love You" from the open bell of his golden horn.

The bratwursts were crispy-brown and puffy from being grilled and were on toasted buns buried beneath heaping mounds of smoldering sauerkraut. Amy bit into hers and savored its sour sweetness. "Wonderful," she said. She followed the bite with a long drink of beer, not a sip like most women.

Noble said, "It is okay for you to eat these? I mean, well . . . you know— ?"

"Because I'm a Jew?" He wished he hadn't said this and it showed on him painfully. She pulled him quickly from the bottom of his embarrassment. "Please, I'm not offended. Not in the least."

"It was a stupid thing to say."

"No, it wasn't. It was real. Most men I know tiptoe around the subject like I'm breakable glass. I wish people would stop it. It's all so silly and unnecessary. And, besides, the bratwurst they serve here is veal."

"That goes to show what I know. I just figured all bratwurst was pork."

She laughed, carefully patting a sparkle of

Getting Sentimental over You

lacy foam from her upper lip with a paper napkin. "I'm afraid not. And, even if it were, I'd still eat it. Although I'd never tell my father."

"Oh."

"He's very strict on the matter. Orthodox. Old fashioned and impossible on the subject, I'm afraid. My whole family's this way. I don't know where I stand." She paused in deep, somber thought for a moment before expelling the subject with an easy wave of fingers. "Anyway, it's a wonderful sandwich."

He looked at her sitting there. She was a special, elegant thing who brought class even to this plain and ordinary setting. "Funny, you know."

"About what?"

"About us. Here we were, in the same class, day after day, right there under each other's noses."

"Not really. We were different people. At least I was, anyway. Oh, my, was I ever." She threw her head back and rolled her eyes in a faking of agony. "Besides, you seemed to be real involved with Audry McClure."

"We went steady all during our senior year."

"What happened?"

"I don't know. The thing just wore itself out, I guess. I think we just both got tired of . . ." He rotated his hand back and forth as a way of saying, "Oh, you know."

She knew. "Got tired of being in each other's pockets."

"Yeah, like that. Exactly. But we're still really good friends. She's a good kid. She's okay. And she's the—"

"Please. I know, I know. You don't have to say it. And the best dancer in Cincinnati."

He couldn't keep from laughing. "C'mon. I wasn't going to say that. And besides, being a good dancer isn't everything."

"No, but it sure can't hurt. I wish I were." Then, in a soft, serious tone, she said, "The last thing I want to do is embarrass you."

She was sincere with this remark. She lowered her sandwich and looked at Noble, and he could sense her insecurity. He took the sandwich from her and placed it on the paper plate in front of her, then took her hands and cupped them in his. "Look. You could never be an embarrassment to me, ever. I'd be proud, privileged to be seen with you anytime, anywhere. And as for dancing . . . well, that's one

Getting Sentimental over You

thing, but it's not that important. What's important between people is what goes on after the music stops."

Amy had read widely, was highly literate and well-educated, but at this moment, surrounded by the cheap-cleaness of this little self-service restaurant, its oilcloth covered tabls coverings and the music of Harry James, she was getting an education.

> *You made me love you,*
> *I didn't wanna do it, I didn't wanna do it . . .**

After eating, they strolled by Lake Como, a large, man-made lake that reflected the park like an abstract watercolor. The periphery of the lake was lined with wooden benches, and on them couples were huddled so close that—in the darkness—they appeared to be one, large, shadowy person.

As Noble and Amy walked in silence near the edge of the lake, Noble thought about the moment and how walking near the lake with

---

Joseph McCarthy. James Monoco. Broadway Music Corp & Sony/ATV Tunes LCC

Amy was different from walking there at other times with other girls. Usually it was all silliness and conversation because silliness and conversation were great warriors in the battle against awkward silence. But on this night, this special night, Noble didn't find the silence awkward at all—he found it strangely comforting. The silence was good. The night knew it was good, the lake knew it was good, and the stars winked their approval of the quietness between them.

Amy, too, had never felt as comfortable with a man. She usually dated men from college who, like her, shared the common interests of plays and books and poetry. It was always, "Have you read this fellow Hemingway?" "What do you think of Proofrock?" "Is it true that Joyce was introverted and sexless?" It was stuff like this that usually accompanied her on dates, stuff of literature and the arts, stuff that required thought and a bit of mental fencing on her part. While stimulating, it was, at the same time, a bit tiring, boring, and certainly not fun.

About halfway around the lake, they found an abandoned bench, seated themselves, and sat looking into the lake and the park that was

Getting Sentimental over You

wet paint on its surface.

"It all seems so far away," she said. "Kind of like it isn't real."

"I guess."

"You think maybe we're dreaming it?"

"How do you mean?"

"I think that sometimes, when things seem perfect, it's all some kind of dream."

"You think?"

"Maybe this is our Nirvana, right here in this park with all the colors and sounds and everything. Maybe today, for whatever reason, we've been taken out of ourselves."

"Hey. Don't go getting deep on me. I'm just a guy with an old Ford and eight sport coats."

"Don't sell yourself short." Then she said, "It's like when everything disruptive is put outside and stays there like you've shut a door on it, and here you are in this place where everything's pure and full of wonder and beauty. This whole day's been like that."

"Yeah. I think I know what you mean. And you're right. This whole day has been kinda like a dream, I guess." He thought about her approaching him on the top deck of the *Island Queen*. "And it all started the moment we met today. It was like . . . I don't know how to express it. In fact, maybe it's better if I don't try. Why try to explain something that's good? You do that, you lose it, you mess it up."

She looked at him with admiration for the perception of his remark. "See, I told you not to sell yourself short."

"You're right, you know, this may be a dream. But I can't dig into it. And why should we? I mean, why spoil it by thinking it to death? I remember once—when I was just a kid—asking my mom about these roses she used to grow. Real pretty. Beautiful and big. We were living up near Middletown at the time. When I asked her why they were so pretty, she said, 'Just because they are.' I thought about this and it made sense to me. So this is the way I've always looked at things and accepted things—for what they are. Like this day. If it's a dream—okay. And when I wake up, that's okay, too. He took her head between his hands and smoothed her hair from her face with easy strokes. "It's like when I look at you, I know you're beautiful and know you're special. I don't have to think about it or try to figure out why. It's like my mom said, it's just because you are. I know it's true because," he splayed his long, tanned fingers over his heart and patted, "because I feel it here."

CHAPTER THIRTEEN

WHEN they arrived at Moonlite Gardens, long lines were snaking from its entrance. A rainbow marquee fronting the ballroom shouted:

TONIGHT! THE TOMMY DORSEY BAND
FEATURING
DICK HAYMES AND THE
SENTIMENTALISTS

There was a feeling of excitement in the movement and shuffling of the crowd, an abounding energy of high expectations. This

Getting Sentimental over You

was a big-time event people had been waiting for for months. From the moment his appearance had been announced and tickets went on sale, they had been hungry for the arrival of T.D. And now, finally, here he was, the Sentimental Gentleman of Swing, the master of the romantic trombone whose glassy tones wrapped themselves around you and made you feel warm and wonderful. It was a time of spectacle, a time to see and feel and move and sway and be—for a few Moonlite hours—swept away. This was Magic. The Big Show. And a grand attraction was soon going to be center ring; the recorded Tommy Dorsey of RCA Victor shellac, the man of many hits—"East of the Sun," "I Guess I'll Have to Dream the Rest," "Stardust"—was soon going to be on the bandstand, live and in person, well-double-breasted-dressed and bigger than his image, bigger than life because he'd be live. With rimless glasses perched low on his nose, he would soon be giving a sentimental downbeat to an evening of dancing and listening under the Ohio sky.

Noble and Amy worked their way through the crowd to the ballroom's entrance, where Noble fished his tickets from his coat pocket and handed them to a capped attendant who took them, tore them in half unceremoniously, and returned the stubs. Then—for the purpose of prompt readmittance—he stamped the backs of their hands with an invisible symbol that would spring luminously, mysteriously, to life under black light. They entered.

Moonlite Gardens ballroom was a large, dreamily lit, embracing lady. Its dance floor, burnished from the buffing of many dancers, reflected the light in a manner that gave it the illusion of a large, hovering platform. Above it was open to the stars and the August night poured in. Around the floor were enough tables and chairs to accommodate 2,500 people—5,000, restless, happy feet.

The bandstand was softly, colorfully, dramatically lighted. Music stands, each bearing the initials TD, ascended from the downstage sax section to trombones through trumpets. Stage-left, an ebony grand showed off her teeth, a bass dozed lazily on its chair, a mother-of-pearl drum set sparkled in the shade of big cymbals. Downstage-right, stiff wooden chairs waited patiently for Dick Haymes and the Sentimentalists. On the stands—lit by low-watt,

Getting Sentimental over You

clear-filament bulbs—was the music (the charts), thick with personal notes and markings and pencil changes and cigarette burns and the wear of repeated thumbings. In these pages lay the magic of Sy Oliver: melody, harmony, tied notes, dotted notes, codas and double bars—the arcana of the music trade. It was all there waiting (the music, the stands, the silent rhythm section), quiescent in the muted glow of multicolored lights, presenting itself to the imagination and heightening anticipation.

The ballroom filled rapidly with people who were intent on being seen, dancing, and—for a few hours—pretending. The tables were quickly occupied and stocked proprietarily with 3.2% beer. Bottles of Coke, 7-Up, and club soda stood by benignly in crimped metal hats. The crowd was all movement and shifting and laughing and excited, out for a big night. And dressed for it.

Women in empire- and princess-styled dresses of polished cotton and organdy tossed off laughs with frivolous cigarette waves. Patent-leather pumps shone at the end of nylon seams. Shiny barrettes pinned back long, side-parted hair. Many were nicely underdressed in short-sleeved blouses, straight skirts, and spectator shoes. Some wore their corsages on their wrists while others had clipped them Lamouresqely in their hair. And, of course, there were the bobby-soxers in their white, tailored blouses, loafers, and the short, pleated skirts that advertised their Shirley Temple knees.

Many of the men wore the popular two-color, two-fabric loafer coats, pockets patched and open, casual and boxy, some in cardigan style. Some wore wide, pleated trousers and double-flapped-pocket sport shirts buttoned at the neck. Long, initialed key chains drooped from belt loops and snaked surreptitiously into pockets. Six-button, double-breasted suits with saber lapels over shirts fronted by arborescent ties gave an air of formality to others, setting them apart as "dudes." Then there were the "cats," the "hepsters," the guys who knew what was happening, Jackson. They were well beyond the front lines of fashion in baggy, severely draped pants that were so tight at the bottoms one wondered how they ever got them over their feet. Their wide-brimmed porkpie hats, stiletto-tipped shoes, their suits with yard-

Getting Sentimental over You

wide shoulders with skirts to the knees zooted them past the avant-garde of dress into the stratosphere of weirdness. Interspersed were soldiers and sailors who were aberrant among the faddishly attired.

After staking out their tables, people moved to the bandstand, where they jockeyed for position in front of it. They pushed and shoved, and craned necks, and rose on tiptoes in order to obtain a better view of their musical heroes, men and women, who—for the most part—lived in radios, fan magazines, and the imagination.

Then, from behind the bandstand, as if on cue, the musicians poured in with swaggering confidence, looking like central casting in their maroon bolero jackets and black tuxedo pants. Each (with the exception of the drummer, bassist, guitar player, and piano man) carried a trophy of polished brass. The crowd surged with a great, squeezing moan, carrying Noble and Amy forward with it. People could be seen standing on their chairs.

The players took their positions. Saxes were secured from neck-straps, trombone slides were spritzed, trumpets' valves were loosened with quick finger flutters. The bass player woke his sleeping instrument with an alarm of low plucks as the drummer pushed a spread of wires from his rubber-covered brushes in preparation of painting the head of his snare, while the guitar man studied frets with his left hand.

Dick Haymes and the Sentimentalists made their entrance quickly and seated themselves on the stiff chairs. Haymes was tall and tanned and immaculate in an ivory-white dinner jacket, every bit as glamorous as his promotional glossy on the easel out front.

Noble was up to the minute with respect to bands and their personnel. He said, "Dick Haymes just replaced Sinatra. Frank [the first-name reference was delivered in a manner that gave the impression he knew him personally] left the band in July."

Then, at last, the arrival of the Master.

Tommy Dorsey loomed from behind the trumpets at the top of the bandstand—a dominating figure. Shouts and applause burst forth in tribute, out of respect and admiration for the man responsible for a hundred recordings, Buddy Rich, Jo Stafford, The Modernaires,

Getting Sentimental over You

Frank Sinatra, and a million small-town dreams. He was a nickel generator for the country's quarter-million jukeboxes, a marcher at the head of "The Hit Parade," a gem in the crown of RCA Victor, a weaver of romance, a reason for people dancing in living rooms and gyms and ballrooms and supper clubs and roadside cafés, and a much-needed diversion from the stark realities of World War II. Tommy Dorsey was The Man—the All-American Music Machine.

Trombone in hand, he made his way down to the front of the band, where he stood in his polar-white gabardine, padded- shoulder, loosely fitting, wrinkle-free suit. (Had it been pressed on his body?) He was beyond impeccable, the man was ice cream just out of the freezer. His black hair was combed straight back and lubricated to shoe-shine brightness. The white buck wing-tips on his feet gave Noble a twinge of envy. He was relaxed and statuesque and exuded leadership. He was in charge and everybody knew it, especially the band members who sat poised and rigid, waiting for the downbeat, respectful of their boss's talent and authority. One didn't malinger or make mistakes in the Tommy Dorsey band, because Tommy Dorsey was a musical perfectionist. It was all business with T.D., and the customer was always right.

With a loose wrist, he moved the trombone's slide several times while making a quarter turn toward the band. Then he placed the mouthpiece to his lips and played the first four notes of his theme song, "I'm Getting Sentimental over You." On the fifth note, he brought the trombone down with an emphatic slash, triggering a full dominant chord, releasing the band. Cheers swelled and subsided and the music rose, the trombone's silken tones soaring above it all. Below him, his fans swayed under his spell, and even though it was warm, they didn't notice because he was making music that was cool. Above them, the man in glasses, this business man with a horn, head slightly tilted, relaxed, shot a brass arrow over the crowd, his message pure and comforting to a sea of dreamy eyes.

Noble pulled Amy from the crowd to an open area of the dance floor. Feeling her tense slightly, sensing her nervousness, he placed his arm around her waist and steadied her gently.

Getting Sentimental over You

His firm tenderness, the feel of his athletic body against hers, relaxed her, gave her self-confidence. She felt safe in his embrace. Then he took her right hand and extended it in his left. Then he began to move ever so slightly in time with the music, swaying metronomically with it in perfect tempo.

Amy had never felt comfortable on the dance floor before, but now, inexplicably, she felt strangely at ease and not self-conscious. Then quickly, deftly, he swept her backward with a long gliding slide that was effortless and performed in perfect sync with a crescendo of music. It left her breathless. Then, unexpectedly, he swung steeply to the left in a half-pirouette, shifting his weight in the opposite direction at the end of a maneuver that was high risk and wonderful.

He knew this music, every beat of it, every change and lyric, and his dancing was an extension of it. And it showed. In contrast to others on the floor, Noble was a professional and, as a result, his partner became better than herself in his arms. She was part of it too, connected, sailing along with him, riding his tide. In Noble's arms, as the man with the horn broadcast his brilliance over the ballroom in muted slides, filling the place with tingles of feeling, she, Amy Fox—the reluctant wallflower—was a dancer. Suddenly, miraculously, there on the floor, her life became music and time a tied note.

The dance floor was now full and alive, a pulsating thing, throbbing with dancers who, with dash and originality, brought their personal élan to the floor. Noble spun Amy among them, guiding her in and out, carving a path for them in the swirling density of body-locked couples. And Amy's confidence grew as they danced, as she followed the intricacies of his lead. She was filled with exhilaration and disbelief. Could this be her? Were her feet actually touching the floor?

Inspired by her ability to respond to him, Noble dug into his repertoire of steps, gradually increasing the difficulty of his maneuvers, which she followed unerringly. They were now one, the two of them, joined inexorably, a single thing communicating through touch and intuition and feeling.

At the end of his silken, golden chorus, Tommy Dorsey stepped aside and Dick Hay-

Getting Sentimental over You

mes took the microphone. His deep-bottom baritone was honey-smoothed over the crowd:

> *Never thought I'd fall,*
> *But now I hear love's call,*
> *I'm getting sentimental over you.*
>
> *Things you say and do,*
> *Just thrill me through and through,*
> *I'm getting sentimental over you . . .*

Then it happened like flash-paper in a magician's hand. Poof! The feelings that had been there from the moment of their meeting on the top deck of the *Island Queen,* every minute element of their day was instantaneously drawn down into a concentrated montage of flashing imagery: the sun; the pool; clothing; the park, its colors and sounds; him on the high-board; her hair; his walk; her voice; his smile; her lean body; the relaxed easiness of his manner; the warmth of her eyes; soft touches and sun-burn smells; talk small and serious; the boardwalk and bratwurst; and Lake Como and Sunlite and Moonlite, sights and sounds and smells—a thousand, memorable impressions were bound permanently in the scrapbook of their minds.

I thought I was happy, I could live without love,
Now I must admit, love is all that I'm thinking of . . .

As Dick Haymes sang the bridge in harmony with the Sentimentalists, Noble stopped dancing. There in the middle of the ballroom, surrounded by dancers, he just stopped. He placed his arms about Amy and held her. Nothing was said between them. At that moment, words were obsolete. They stood looking at each other. They were alone. Oblivious. At that moment, Coney Island didn't exist: there were no dancers, no music—nothing. Their emotions erased the slate. They both knew—there was no question about it, no avoiding it—that they had fallen in love.

Noble placed his hands behind her head, cupping it carefully. Then he pulled her up to him and kissed her. As their lips lingered, the band jumped to the coda with a rising wail of chromatics, filling Moonlite and masking the distant, tin-pan sounds of the park. And T.D.

slid in under the moment, solidifying it, capturing it forever in his web of golden tones.

They were still kissing when the band segued into "Stardust."

The remainder of the evening was danced in silence to ballads and jive. What was there to say? Nothing. Their eyes did the talking, saying more in their recesses than a thousand shouted words. Their love was an unspoken thing coming from behind that low wall in the garden of their desires.

At the end of the night, as the band reprised its theme and the trombone took its final slides, they kissed again, sealing the evening with bliss.

As the crowd was drained from the ballroom, Amy and Noble broke away to enjoy the Lake Como fireworks, a nightly, crowning event rewarding those who stayed till the park shut down. They seated themselves in the grass near the edge of the lake. Amy pulled on her cashmere sweater. Noble placed his arm around her and pulled her close to him, and she snuggled against him, leaning her head against his shoulder. He smelled the distinctive essence of her perfume, felt the errant strands of her night-damp hair against his cheek.

The first rocket was air-mailed skyward, reaching its apex with a loud burst from which a shower of stars rained downward in a cascade of rapid, silver explosions. Then, in fast succession, came a series of high-reaching red streaks that culminated in loud puffs of iridescent fireflowers, seeming to pop out of the sky like someone had stuck pins in it. The fireworks display, reflected in the lake (making the show a double-feature), ended with a rapid, overlapping statement of patriotic thunder.

After the fireworks, the park cleared, and the rides were put to rest. Cars streamed from the parking lot, bug-eyed-sleepy and sluggish. Another Coney Island day had ended.

Noble and Amy joined the crowd walking the path to the Rivergate landing.

At the landing, the *Island Queen* waited, looking more regal than she did during the day because she was outlined with lights and lit warmly inside. The river squished softly against her hull with the regularity of a wet time machine, rocking her a bit as her passengers boarded, Amy and Noble among them. After the passengers had boarded, ropes were

Getting Sentimental over You

cast off, and the band began to play "Moonlight Serenade"—fitting launch music for the return trip to Cincinnati. The boat backed to center stream, reversed, and lurched forward, its big side-paddles roiling the water to a moonlight froth.

On the final return trip to Cincinnati, the top deck of the *Queen* was referred to as the lovers' deck because this is where they congregated to embrace and plan and dream. And this was where Noble took Amy, up to the top deck, the lovers' deck, where they stood at the rail, gazing off into the river darkness. Below, they could hear the water breaking against the hull and the clarinet's reedy shrillness as it took the lead on the second chorus of "Moonlight Serenade." They said nothing, they just looked and listened and absorbed. They had been virtually silent since "I'm Getting Sentimental Over You," and remained so for a long time there on the top deck, the lovers' deck.

"I never knew how good it could be," she said. "How special."

She was all textures beside him, all feminine and silky and cashmere. "Yes," he said. "Life's a crazy thing, isn't it? You never know where it's going to lead. You think you're safe, you're walking along on this little path and then, alluva sudden, there's an unexpected turn."

She raised her eyes to his. "It's been a special day. Perfect. And we'll always have it, no matter what happens."

"What could happen?"

"I don't know. It just all seems so unreal. Like it's too good to be true."

He took her by her arms at the elbows and turned her toward him. "Look at me. It's real. Everything about it, from the time you came up to me on the trip up the river till right now. It's all been real, every minute of it. Real and special. And beautiful, just like you."

And she was. And more. There in the frosty glow from the many bulbs that traced the boat's silhouette, she was also an alluring, desirable woman. Noble kissed her again—her lips, her cheeks, the soft, tanned skin of her neck. And she complied, offering herself freely.

They remained on the top deck until the lights of Cincinnati came booming up from behind the long sweep of River Bend. Then they went below to the ballroom, where they danced as the *Queen* narrowed the gap between them

Getting Sentimental over You

and the end of their day. Amy was relaxed in his arms, following his every lead as if they'd been partners for years. It now all seemed so easy for her, so right. For Noble, too. Perhaps he'd been with better dancers, perhaps Audry McClure could outshine her with subtle nuances and refinements, but Amy was heaven in his arms because she was beyond steps and moves and twirls, beyond the music, beyond all of this in an elevating, spiritual way.

They continued to dance till the band wound down "Stairway to the Stars" and the boat slid to the landing at the foot of Broadway, where it was eased into its moorings with preciseness and care. The ramp was lowered and people poured ashore; a much more subdued group than the animated, bumptious, family crowd that had accompanied Noble and Amy up the river earlier in the day. They commented on this as they walked arm-in-arm up the gentle slope leading from the landing to the parking area.

At the roadster, Noble kissed Amy again before seating her in the car. Then he raised the car's top and secured it because—even though it was August—this time of night carried a damp chill. Especially near the river. They pulled from the parking area in a spread-hand of traffic whose fingers pointed to the streets of Vine, Elm, Walnut, Broadway, and Sycamore. As they headed up Broadway, Noble snapped on the radio, and Glen Gray and his Casa Loma Orchestra serenaded them with "Memories of You." Then he placed his arm around Amy and pulled her across the wide bench seat until she was next to him. She placed her head on his shoulder and nuzzled into him, burying herself in his masculine warmness.

Accompanied by "Memories of You," they turned up Reading Road in the direction of Bond Hill. The street was quiet and deserted, the only intruder being the Ford's V-8 as it snored lazily in third gear. A bus, stopped at an intersection, dispensed a single passenger, ejecting him from its amber-lit interior to the late-darkness of Saturday night.

Near the top of Reading Road, as Bunny Berigan reached for the high notes of "I Can't Get Started," Noble turned into one of Bond Hill's residential side streets, then made another quick turn onto the street where Amy lived. There were no street lights, and it was

Getting Sentimental over You

dark, and the Ford's headlamps swept the darkness with long, probing eyes. Large, overhanging maples with sap-smelling leaves created a long tunnel under which they drove. The big houses in the neighborhood were asleep, save an occasional lit window indicating insomnia within. Noble slid the Ford to the curb fronting Amy's house and killed its engine and Bunny Berigan.

They sat in silence for a long time, Amy still nestled tightly against him. It was dark and quiet and restful under the musty smelling maples, the maples of summer. The only sounds were the low hummings of insects and the occasional, distant bark of a restless dog. Noble turned and looked down at Amy and she met his gaze as if anticipating it. There was hesitation. Then he said, "I love you, Amy."

Time poured slowly into the pause created by his pronouncement, by his three small words that offered vulnerability and commitment. These were words not to be said or taken lightly. Amy knew this and thought deeply about it before replying, "And I love you too, Noble."

And there, under the low maples on that

long-ago Saturday night in August, a bond was forged, a bond of love was welded and sanctified by the exchange of three, profoundly simple words.

CHAPTER FOURTEEN

AUGUST 2, 1988

THE lemonade had long been drunk, and it was now late. The evening and the beverage had run out as Kris and I sat listening to Noble's story of that eventful day way back in 1942. He had told his story well, clearly and with feeling, unfolding it with skillful exposition, and the imagery of it lingered at the conclusion of his telling. But it was incomplete. It had been sharply truncated, leaving us in great anticipation of knowing what had happened beyond that night under the maples. But Noble lapsed into silence, looking off in a detached way, offering no further information. And we, as a consequence, were left dry and unfulfilled.

Kris and I sat for a while in silence. After all, what could we say? But his story demanded clarification, completeness. Kris finally cut through the heaviness of the moment. "Noble," she said, "that was beautiful." There was no response. He just kept looking off into the night like there was something to see beyond the trees on the other side of the street. "It was a beautiful story," she persisted, "but what happened then?"

Again silence. Had we lost the battle? Were the events beyond too painful for recalling? Apparently this was the case, because he continued to study the distance with a fixed gaze. At the risk of being rude, I spoke his name forcefully. "Noble!" He stirred, blinking his eyes as if awakening from a long slumber, returning to focus. "I'm sorry. I didn't mean to shock you."

He was back with us and apologetic. "Oh, no. No. That's okay. It was . . . it was just . . . " he hesitated, again lapsing slightly, "the memories are—a bit too much, that's all."

Getting Sentimental over You

Kris leaned forward, placing her hand on his knee. "We understand. And after all, it's really none of our business."

"Right," I said.

"It's just that the story is so wonderful, so sweet. And then you leave us hanging," she said.

"I understand," he said. "It was rude of me to cut you off like that. I'm sorry. It's just that . . . well, it's just that beyond that point the story gets . . ."

"Look," Kris said, "you don't owe us an explanation. Let's drop it, okay?

Then he surprised us. "But I want you to know, I think it's important. I don't mean in any earth-shaking way, but important for me to finally get it out, talk about it, get it all out after all these years. No, no—I wanna tell you."

And he did:

"Well, we were both crazy about each other, crazy in love. And for the next five months, right up through the holidays, we saw each other every day. And when we weren't together, we were talking on the phone. I can't tell you how very much I loved her. There aren't words in any poem or dictionary or any book ever written that could express how I felt about that girl. I was just plain nuts about her.

"Anyway, we went together through the holidays, and in January we were engaged. Now, I know it all sounds real smooth, but there was a problem. A big one. Her father. He was an Orthodox Jew who was set on Amy marrying one of his kind. Although he treated me okay, he was always distant and kinda cool. And then there was this big social difference and this big gap in education. Amy was downright brilliant, could go anywhere. Me? Well . . . I was just a good-looking jock with a defense job and a hot car. Her dad resented this. Not that he came right out and said anything. But you could tell.

"Then there was something even bigger. The war. Hell, I mean, I just couldn't ignore it anymore. Even though I was doing defense work, doing my part, this still didn't cut it. I had to get in. I wanted to get in. So I enlisted. Amy and I had one helluva battle over it. Almost broke us up. But I explained to her that I just couldn't live with myself sitting on the sidelines. If I hadn't met Amy, I'd enlisted sooner. She wanted to get married right away, but it

Getting Sentimental over You

wouldn't have been realistic. Hell . . . I could become a statistic on some beach somewhere. So I convinced her it would be crazy. It was the proper thing to do, and I'd do it again. She said she'd wait. So we got engaged. When she told her dad, he went crazy. It sure didn't come as a surprise. I knew I wasn't his idea of the perfect son-in-law.

"I went into the Army in June of 1943, did my basic at Fort Dix, and was shipped overseas on August 2, one year to the day that Amy and I had met on the *Island Queen.* Only this time there wasn't any Tommy Dorsey, there was just a dirty troop transport and a date with some unknown Germans and Italians. Amy and I talked on the phone every day while I was in camp, and communicated by V-mail almost as often while I was in Europe. I was in the middle of some pretty rough scrapes over there and would have gone crazy without her letters.

"Well, the rest is almost a cliché, I guess. Nothing new, that's for sure. After about a year or so, her letters began to trickle off and the ones I received were losing their personal quality, the sweetness. It got to the point where they were almost like nothing more than letters from a good friend. Then came the final blow, the brutal blow.

"It came during the Battle of the Bulge after I'd been reassigned to the 7th Armored Division. We'd just held off Detrich's 6th Panzer Army at St. Vith and were resting up and waiting for orders. We got mail call." He took the cigar box from the metal stand, opened it, and carefully withdrew faded pages that had been folded so many times they were separating at the creases. "Here's the letter I got that day from Amy."

My dearest Noble:

I have been putting off writing this letter for some time because the last thing in the world I want to do is hurt you. But I just didn't know how to avoid it any longer. I'm sure it will reach you at the worst possible time, but delaying what I have to say will only compound the injury.

I have, through the tone of my recent letters, attempted to soften the impact of this message. I know this sounds cowardly, but I do care deeply for you and, well, if this makes me a coward, so be it.

Now, before I go farther, I want you to know that I do love you and that you will always hold a great part of me. But there are factors that transcend love, my darling. I know this will be difficult for you to understand because our backgrounds are so vastly different. When we first met, and during those wonderful intervening months before you went away, I had convinced myself that my Jewishness was of little importance. I mean, after all, I'm a modern, educated woman. When my father so adamantly objected to our marriage, I was greatly upset with him for his narrowness, his hide-bound adherence to (what I thought were) superstition and Old World ways. But over time, I have come to realize that a marriage between us would ultimately be a bad thing, that my father was right.

I'm sure you're wondering why this shift in attitude. Well, the realities of this war, the heinous acts of persecution, murder, and debasement of my people have greatly changed my opinions and rekindled and solidified within me my allegiance with, and feelings for, Jews and the orthodox traditions of our religion. And even though the war has served to magnify these feelings, I am now convinced that they had lain dormant within me, were always there by virtue of background, Temple and parenting. Therefore, my dearest Noble, as much as it pains me to tell you, a marriage between us is impossible. I've thought this through completely, agonized over it, debated it, and I always come to the same conclusion, so don't attempt to change my mind.

If, once in their lifetime, a person knows real love, he is blessed. Well, my dearest, we have had that experience, and whatever happens in our brief moment on this planet, we will always have Coney Island and our beautiful, unforgettable day in the sun. When I think about it, and I do daily, it all comes back vividly, the sights and sounds and smell of that special, once-in-a-lifetime day. I can recall you plainly standing there next to the railing on the top deck of the Island Queen, the wind and the sun framing you in all your gentle handsomeness. Every moment of that August day, every texture of it is a picture I run often in my mind. But the highlight, the golden moment, was there on the dance floor, under the stars, when you swept me away to the music of Tommy Dorsey. The memory is chilling in it's delight. And the memory and the music will never fade.

Be well, darling, and may God protect and look after you out there, wherever you are. And please remember, I'll always be sentimental over you.
Love,
Amy

Getting Sentimental over You

After he stopped reading, we allowed the silence to linger. He refolded the letter, placed it in the box, and returned the box to the metal stand. We said nothing. What could anyone say at a time like this? We could only, in our removed and impersonal way, attempt to grasp at the edges of his sadness. We could never know how he felt, we could only have unspoken sympathy for this emotionally injured man.

We were relieved when he finally said, "Well, there you have it. This is the reason I never married. I should have gotten over it, I guess, but the rejection, and the loss were just too hurtful. I know it seems kind of extreme, but this is the way it affected me." Noting tears in Kris's eyes, he said, "Sorry. Didn't mean to upset you."

"It's not that, it's just so—damned sad."

"I guess I was just a sentimental young fool who didn't have the good sense to get over it. And now I'm a sentimental old one who still hasn't."

"You don't have to make excuses."

"Kris is right," I added.

"And you never saw her after that?"

"Nope."

"Never?"

"Never. I could have. After I was discharged, I returned to Cincinnati. But it wouldn't have been right. I never heard from her, either. Then I went to college on a GI bill and, from what I was told at the time, Amy got involved with the Zionist movement and went off to Israel. Last I heard she was living in New York City. Her husband was killed in the Six Days War."

"And there's been no contact?"

"None. It wouldn't be a good idea. I've even avoided the class reunions for this reason. Fact is, we've got our fiftieth coming up in September. The 17th."

"Fiftieth? Wow! That's a biggie."

"All it means to me is that I'm sixty-seven years old."

"You're not going?"

"No."

She couldn't believe this. "To your fiftieth high-school reunion?"

"No."

"You've got to go."

"Why?"

Getting Sentimental over You

"Everybody does."

"Not this everybody."

"Aren't you the least bit curious?"

"Of course. Sure. But I'm still not going."

"Because of Amy, right?"

"Yes."

"But would it be better if—"

"No!" This was the first time he'd expressed irritation. Then, realizing he'd snapped at her, he softened his tone. "It wouldn't be better at all. It would be awful. Some things are better off left buried."

I was surprised at Kris. This wasn't like her. She normally didn't involve herself in the personal matters of others and referred to people who did as "buttinskys."

"Mr. Johnson—Noble—I think you're making a terrible mistake." He attempted to interrupt, but she stopped him with a raised hand. "Please . . . let me finish. Look, I know it's none of my business, I know I'm probably way off base here, but, even at the risk of upsetting you, I've got to tell you what I think, okay?" He settled back grudgingly, scrunching down in his chair self-protectively into a resistant cocoon. "This business of avoiding seeing her is not healthy. In fact, it only makes matters worse. You just can't go on living inside that little box for the rest of your life. Look how much you've lost already. Here you are, a healthy, good-looking man sitting around inside of memories, bound up in the past, reliving something that happened forty-some years ago. I loved your story. It was beautiful, touching. But it's also damned sad. Sad for you, because you're trapped in it. And now here you have a chance, maybe a last chance, to see Amy and talk and reminisce and relive all those happy moments, and you're throwing it all away, going to blow it because you're afraid."

After thinking about this for a moment, he said, "Or maybe because I'm just plain stubborn."

"I think it's more than that," she said. "But whatever the reason, you should put it aside and go to that reunion, because seeing her will be a healing thing. Believe me. It'll be a way of coming to grips, getting things behind you, facing up, putting the past to rest."

He pondered her remarks for a few seconds, running his tongue thoughtfully around the inside of his cheeks. You could almost hear his

Getting Sentimental over You

think-clock ticking, see its pendulum swinging in the deepness of his contemplation. "You know, Kris, you may be right. Everything you say may be right on the money. But I'm not going. It's outta the question."

His response was firm and put a cap on the subject as well as the evening (pursuing the issue would have been highly improper). So we said our good-byes, thanking him for his hospitality, his story, the music, and the deliciously refreshing lemonade under the magnolia's low ceiling.

CHAPTER FIFTEEN

AUGUST *dragged on, bringing its heat and humidity and mornings of haze-covered sun. Lawns were brown and hard, and the trees pleaded for rain, their withered leaves upturned in supplication.*

Then August stepped aside like a gentleman for September, who entered hot and bothered before settling down into cooler, shorter, dryer days with high western skies filled with show-off sunsets. Kids were back in school, leaves were dying into beauty, coffee tasted better in the morning, and I was back on campus attempting to teach theater to kids whose minds were on the

Getting Sentimental over You

drama of football.

During the intervening weeks, since our evening with him under his magnolia tree, we had seen little of Noble Johnson. Other than an exchange of occasional waves, glimpsing him as he backed his Buick from his garage, or seeing him working in his yard, our contact had been limited. On the couple of occasions when Kris had taken him chocolate-chip cookies, he had accepted them with gratitude, but had not invited her in or engaged her in extended conversation. And when she had asked him to come for dinner, he demurred, claiming a previous engagement. Kris blamed herself for this. She felt she had overstepped her bounds, had strayed far from the course of propriety by offering advice on that eventful evening of August 2nd. She felt rotten about it. She was contrite, up to the brim with blame for upsetting him. This is why she was greatly relieved when he showed up at our door on the cracker-crisp morning of September 17th.

The young man with the impressive collection of shoes and a closet hung meticulously with the best his paycheck could buy had lost none of his flair for clothing. At our door that morning he was as advertised—beautifully tailored and accoutered: a navy pin-stripe, two-button suit; white, highly starched, spread-collar, French-cuffed shirt with small, discrete links; an amethyst, silk necktie; suede lace-up shoes. His hair was combed straight back and shiny, its highlights like hammered silver. He was a study in sartorial correctness, a page torn from an *Esquire* of the thirties, a vintage cover from *Cutter and Tailor*, a still from *Flying Down to Rio*. He turned our front doorway into a storefront window, placing himself as a handsome mannequin at its center. But there was no stiffness to him. He was at ease.

"Don't you have a minute?" he asked.

"Sure, sure. Of course." He stepped into the room, upgrading it with a presence of elegance.

"Is Kris around?"

"Yeah. She's in the kitchen. Hold on, I'll get her. Sit down. Make yourself at home." Kris was hands-deep in batter, in the process of turning one of her mysteries into an edible museum piece. "It's Mr. Johnson—Noble."

"Oh, my, look at me." She swiped a hair that wasn't out of place from her forehead, adding another eyebrow of flour. "What's he want?"

Getting Sentimental over You

As I thumbed the flour from her forehead, I said, "I don't know. But he looks like a million bucks. Maybe he's come over to propose. And if he has, you'll accept."

"God, I look awful," she said, untying her apron, slipping it over her head.

He was as pleased by her entrance as she was obviously astounded by his appearance. "Noble. Good morning. Excuse my appearance." She fumbled with her apron, wiping her hands on it. "I was just whipping up an apple pie."

"You look fine."

"And look at you. My!"

"Is this a bad time? I didn't mean to—"

"No, no. Not at all."

"I just wanted to come over and give you some news. And apologize."

"Apologize? For what?"

"For the way I've been acting lately. Isn't like me, really. I've just had a whole lot of thinking to do, that's all."

Kris had a mountain of stockpiled contrition. "No. I think I'm the one who should be apologizing here. For speaking up like I did, I mean. I shouldn't have. It was none of my business. I couldn't blame you for being upset."

He laughed, relieving the solemnity of her expression. "I wasn't upset. No way. Not in the least. Really. In fact, I'm glad you did. It got me to thinking. Everything you said made a heck of a lot of sense. I needed it, needed the push. That's the reason I came over. I wanted to tell you that I'm going to the reunion. "

"You aren't!"

"I am."

"Really?"

"Yep."

"Fantastic," Kris said.

I was just as enthusiastic. "Noble, that's great."

"Wonderful. You'll be the best lookiggone there," Kris added.

"You think."

"You kidding? Look at you."

"Well, thanks," he said with a shy, twisted grin. "I'm leaving early because I wanna get down there and take a look around. Old places. Memories, and that, you know."

Kris cupped his hand in hers. "I think it's just terrific," she said. "Whatever happens, it'll be a terrific experience."

Getting Sentimental over You

"I guess. I don't know. I'm not putting any expectations on it. I just thought that, you know . . . well . . . I can't run forever."

There were obvious questions to be asked, but we withheld them. It was special moment of silently shared feelings and projected thoughts of events ahead. Noble Johnson, the silent one, our good neighbor, was about to set sail on an adventure too complex to chart, a trip on a sea of a thousand memories and regrets.

Later, he told us this story . . .

CHAPTER SIXTEEN

SATURDAY, SEPTEMBER 17, 1988

THE Hughes High School 50th Class Reunion was held at the Vernon Manor Hotel at Oak and Burnet Streets in Cincinnati, Ohio. The Vernon Manor was, at one time, an old residential hotel catering to Cincinnati's finest and frequented by little ladies in big hats who took lunch there in its gussied-up dining room, indulging themselves in finger sandwiches and local scuttlebutt. The hotel was still posh and exclusive due to complete renovation and now used often for the purpose of reunions and similar functions.

Getting Sentimental over You

After touring the city, Noble arrived at the Vernon Manor in the early evening and parked behind the hotel. He entered the hotel and went to the ballroom. At the entrance to the ballroom there were long tables arrayed with rectangular ID cards in plastic holders. The cards were presented alphabetically, and on each was the attendee's name and class photo. On the back of the plastic holders were safety pins to accommodate the attaching to dress or lapel. Behind the table was a once-cute, now overweight and matronly classmate who greeted him and handed him a 50th Anniversary, Hughes High School, Class of 1938 booklet and assigned him a table. He located his ID and signed the register. A lapel puncture would have been unthinkable, so Noble draped his ID from the breast pocket of his pinstriped suit.

Upon entering the ballroom, Noble was greeted by an outpouring of handshakes and hugs and fraternal backslaps that greatly relieved his tensions and apprehensions. He was still the admired one, their Adonis, the jock who was the David who slew a thousand competitive lions. While he was shocked at the appearance of many and impressed by the appearance of a few, he wasn't inordinately shocked or surprised, because he knew that age was a capricious thing, that it played favorites. He was thankful for being one of its pets.

The ballroom was large, impersonal and brightly lit. Round, linen-covered tables, looking like silver-set lily pads, floated around the room and large black numbers identifying each grew from their centers on chrome-plated stems. There was a dance floor and a riser for the band.

Old pals, past-tense dates and tacit acquaintances presented a gauntlet, one to be politely overcome, so it took Noble some time to reach his assigned table. But he didn't mind—he was enjoying himself, finding the occasion—contrary to what he'd anticipated—one of pleasant renewal. He was gratified to see his old classmates and they him, and the feelings they shared flowed warmly between them. Old stories were swapped and exaggerated in their recall: past gridiron exploits, pranks, old flames, the wildness of school-time days. There were "how ya beens" and "remember whens" and "whatever happened tos?" There was talk of the war and the many who had served and

Getting Sentimental over You

those who never returned. And, of course, teachers were recalled: Old Man Larsen, who put the all of the pretty girls in the front row; One-Finger Sewell, the careless shop teacher; Miss Rule, the eccentric math teacher whose breath could wilt flowers; "Beer-Belly" Henderson, the obese coach who smelled like the Burger Brewery. It was all recalled with laughter and fond remembrance because it was all yesterday, and yesterday was young and carefree and without mortality. Fifty long ages ago.

They sat and ate rubber chicken and small, hard peas; cold, boiled potatoes; three strips of mushy asparagus; and a salad that had resisted mixing. But the food was secondary. Who really cared? Not this gathering of old people with class photos of somebody else in their plastic holders.

After they had eaten, there were speeches and presentations that were boring and fun.

During the evening, since his entrance, Noble had been reluctant to scan the room thoroughly for Amy. He had trepidation of seeing her. Because of this, he didn't circulate. Although he sensed her presence there somewhere among the hundreds who occupied the big, round tables, he was as yet loath to seek her out. This would come later, after dessert and the speeches and awards were out of the way and the band started to play and people milled and mixed in search of old friends and spiritual rejuvenation.

Near the end of the speeches, he pushed back his melting rainbow sherbet and reached for his 50th Anniversary booklet, the one that had been given him upon arrival. He thumbed casually through its pages, noting names familiar and not, photos and information about Hughes High circa '38: scholastic achievements, sports highlights (his photo was ubiquitous in this section), faculty, humorous bits and pieces. At the back of the booklet was a section headed "In Memory." His eyes dropped down the page. Slowly. The As, the Bs, the Cs. A chill rose within him as his eyes moved down the alphabet toward the land of the Fs. D, E . . . Falter, Finch, Fitzgerald, Flanigan . . . GARY! His heart rose after the safe traverse of the dreaded Fs. There was no Fox. Relieved, he settled back and aimlessly stirred his rainbow sherbet to a vanishing sunset.

Getting Sentimental over You

"Noble!" He felt a hand on his shoulder. "Noble!" The hand shook him slightly. "Noble, it's me. Audry. Audry McClure." He spun around and faced her. She placed her hands on her hips in a gesture of faked impatience and disappointment. "You don't remember?"

"Of course. Of course I remember, Audry. How could I ever forget? Are you kidding? How could I ever forget Audry McClure, Miss Angora Sweaters? And look at you. You look terrific." And she did. She was no longer the racy teen of dirty saddles and pleated skirts and seductive sweaters, but she was an attractive woman, not at all showing her age. And she still had her great dancer's legs.

"You think so?" she said, brightening at his compliment.

"Yes. Absolutely." He stood and took her hands and held her out at arm's length as if displaying her. "You look great—fantastic." He gave her a smothering hug.

"You don't look so bad yourself. For an older man, that is," she added facetiously.

"Please. My! How long's it been, anyhow?"

She had to adjust her mental clock for this one. "God—Forty-five years?"

"Good Lord. I'll bet you have ten grandchildren by now."

"No. Just six."

"Well, you sure don't show it. You look wonderful."

"How about you?"

"Can't claim any."

"Oh."

"Kinda hard when you aren't married."

"You? You're kidding? Divorced?" Then, with embarrassed hesitation, "Or maybe—?"

"Nope. None of the above. Just never made it to the altar."

"You mean to tell me someone who looks like you escaped? My, this is a strange world we live in."

"And you . . . ?"

"Been married over forty years. To Harry Washburn."

"Little Harry Washburn? The skinny guy with freckles?"

"More freckles than hair, these days, I'm afraid."

"Well, I'll be damned. Well . . . he's a lucky man. You still dance?"

"Every Saturday night. Rain or shine." She

Getting Sentimental over You

winked. "With or without Harry."

"Well, you still have the legs for it."

"This is your first, isn't it?"

"Yep. Finally, after fifty years."

"I've been to all of 'em. Pretty much the same. Except every year the crowd gets smaller."

"Yeah. I read the memoriam. Say . . . you ever see Amy Fox?"

She chewed the inside of her mouth thoughtfully. "No. Lost track of her after high school. I was never that close to her anyway. She was a brain. My brains were in my feet."

"She ever attend the reunions?"

"No. None. Not to my knowledge, anyway. Say, you had quite a thing with her, didn't you?" Noble nodded. "Say, come on over and say hi to Harry."

"In a minute. I wanna step out for some fresh air first."

"Okay. Just see you don't get lost. See you in a bit then, all right? I'll save you a dance."

"Sure, Aud." He watched her as she walked away, wondering why someone as vivacious and attractive as Audry would marry a guy like "Freckles" Washburn. Then he smiled to himself. Her remark, "With or without Harry" said it all.

It was obvious, based upon Audry's news, Noble was not going to see Amy Fox now or ever, so he decided to call it a night. For him the party was over. Amy had apparently disappeared into the world harbor of earthly souls. He eased himself around the room, casually exchanging remarks and small-talk, working his way toward the entrance doors to the ballroom. Near the doors he removed his name tag, placed it on a serving tray and turned to exit. As he reached for the doors they opened and there was Amy. They stood facing each other, speechless, frozen.

The room began to spin before him, its sounds shrinking to a dissonant murmur as time and space moved backward over the years to a long-ago day in the sun. And across time, over the transom of a door closed years ago, came vividly the sights and sounds of that special day. Every facet of that diamond Sunday shone like a new-polished stone, every sight and smell and touch and feel came roaring back, spilling out of the past liquid and clear and tangible. The river, the *Queen*, Coney Is-

Getting Sentimental over You

land, and Sunlite Pool. The way she looked at him. Their touches and caresses, fingers intertwined, lips moist and lingering. It was all there, all of it, plain as noon in August. Laughter and secrets told. Dreams shared. Discovery and revelation. The night and the music and the trombone that carried the music to them as they danced. The boat ride and the city coming up like sunrise in the night. And the moment of consecration under the elms; that moment of lover's truth when she replied, "I love you, too, Noble." It came back again and again. "I love you too, Noble. I love you, too . . ."

Amy stepped forward into his arms and they embraced in silence, holding each other tightly, feeling the comforting warmth of the enduring love between them, love that had never died. The years had changed nothing. They were still youthful in their desires. It was still a bright sunshine day, and the river breezes were strong. Then, behind them, as if on cue, as if prompted by a mystical downbeat, the band began to play "I'm Getting Sentimental over You."

And once again they danced.